Adventures
of the
BOOK BATTLING KIDS
-THE CARSON CORNERS CHRONICLES-

Adventures
of the
BOOK BATTLING KIDS
–THE CARSON CORNERS CHRONICLES–

RICHARD BRIAN HARVELL

WATERWOOD PUBLISHING GROUP
CHARLOTTE NC

First edition, 2006

Publisher's Cataloging-in-Publication
(Provided by Quality Books, Inc.)

Harvell, Richard Brian.
Adventures of the book battling kids : the Carson
Corners chronicles / by Richard Brian Harvell. — 1st ed.
    p.   cm.
 SUMMARY: Depression-era children unearth a set of old
books from the town's mercantile and mayhem erupts when
fictional characters, both good and evil, emerge.
 Audience: Ages 9-13.
    LCCN 2005932128
    ISBN 0-9769044-7-0
    ISBN 13: 978-0-9769044-7-2

 1. Depressions—1929—North Carolina—Juvenile fiction. 2. Books and reading—Juvenile fiction. [1. Poverty—Fiction. 2. Depressions—1929—Fiction. 3. Books and reading—Fiction. 4. Fantasy. 5. North Carolina—Fiction.] I. Title.

PZ7.H267445Adv 2006   [E]
        QBI05-600139

Cover illustration by Robert Papp
Cover design by ATG Productions-www.atgproductions.com
Printed in the United States of America

Waterwood Publishing Group
Charlotte, NC 28220
Visit us at www.waterwoodpublishing.com

Acknowledgements

In the spring of 2005, I was telling my mother about the publisher's plan for the book and she said, "It's all so exciting, like a baby being born." I guess like any parent you have to let your children go out into the world, stumble around, fall down, find their own way. Parents have lots of people to thank and I'm no exception. My own mom and dad, grandparents to this endeavor so to speak, have been amazing in offering love, support and advice on a life long level. The editorial talents of Rosanne Catalano and the designers at ATG Productions were awesome and Robert Papp is, hands down, the best cover illustrator on earth! That's my humble opinion, but every time I look at the cover I am awed by his artwork. Errol Lincoln Uys also deserves a nod for his wonderful book, *Riding the Rails: Teenagers on the Move During the Great Depression*. The memories of box-car boys and girls were a source of inspiration and helped me create some of the adventures that Walter, Tex and Jimmy experienced as they bummed around the country.

However, no one was more instrumental in making the book happen than Myron Casey at Waterwood Publishing

Group. He championed the book from the get-go and without his support, drive and belief in the work, there's no way it would have seen the light of day. He's been the book's godfather of sorts; offering advice, financial and emotional support and frankly, I think he loves those kids as much as I do. I also wanted to thank the authors who molded much of my childhood and whose creations (or variations thereof) exist within these pages. By putting my own spin on such classic characters I hope I did justice to the works of Herman Melville, L. Frank Baum, J. M. Barrie, Bram Stoker, Charles Dickens and others.

Finally, I have to say a big thank you to Alice, John, Jimmy, Tex and Walter—the Book Battling Kids themselves. I loved every minute of the time we spent together and I'm as proud as any parent could ever be. It was a grand adventure, but remember when there are no more rails to ride, no more battles to fight, no villains to vanquish, you can come home. The door is always open so sleep tight.

That's it. They're all yours now, but remember to play nice, share and give everyone a turn. Those are the ground rules and you've heard it straight from the Book Battling Kid's father.

Now go on...read...enjoy!

Chapter One

Riding the Rails to Carson Corners

The clickity-clack of the wheels became hypnotic to her as the cars swayed on the tracks of the Seaboard Air Line. Alice Horton sat with her back against the wooden slats of the dirty boxcar, her light brown hair tied in pigtails. Her brother John readjusted his floppy black hat over his blond hair and let out a sigh. They had left the Alabama fields behind them in the dusty shadows of a cold morning with the sky stuffed with stars and a barn owl hooting from the rafters of the horse shed. Now, the sun was starting to break over the ridge of hills outside. Alice pulled her straw hat low on her forehead and tried not to cry. She had left her parents standing in a slice of moonlight and waved from the train car as they faded into the distance.

Alice looked around. The car was filled with hobos, some having a smoke in the open doorway, some stretched out on the floor snoozing, others huddled in the corners laughing and sharing a snort of whiskey or a bit of snuff. A man with a thin line of stubble on his pointy chin was sitting in a corner reading a ragged copy of *Strange Tales of Mystery and Terror* and humming "When It's Springtime in the Rockies." To her right, Alice watched a woman in a thin cotton dress and a black overcoat cradle a baby against the roaring wind. Alice guessed the man beside her was her husband. He stood staring out the train car with a blank look on his face.

Alice rested her head back and tried to sleep while the train rumbled over the tracks. She was proud she had flipped out on her first freight. She had pulled herself up and then reached out into the dark to grab her little brother's hand and hoist him up as the train started rolling. Catching out on the fly was never a good idea. She secretly hoped it would not become a habit. If she never had to hop another train it would suit her just fine. Alice's hand slipped down into the pocket of her father's heavy coat. She felt the bundle of food wrapped up nice and tight: corn pone, fried dough, a small bit of dried beef. If they were careful it would last them until they reached Carson Corners, nestled in the piedmont of North Carolina.

When the stock market had crashed in 1929, her father had lost almost everything. For a while, with her mother bringing in washing and ironing for people around the neighborhood and the odd jobs her father managed to find, they squeezed out a meager living, but it wasn't enough. Last year, they had moved to Alabama to be sharecroppers. There, they lived in a tiny one-room shack made of metal and old boards that let in the wind and the rain. There was no electricity and no running water. Sometimes they only had some fried flour and dirty water for supper.

The summer crops had not been good. Alice's mother, Eunice, had finally written her sister Effigy to ask if Alice and John could come live with her. She begged her sister to take the children in, to give them a home and food until times got better. A letter came back to Eunice Horton with three words scribbled on the fine linen paper: *Let them come.*

Now Alice dreamed of how nice it would be when they arrived and could live with their aunt and had food to eat. No more cramps from the hunger pains. She knew very little about her aunt, Effigy Goode, but couldn't wait to meet her. Something must have strained family relations, because Alice's mother had never talked about her sister until around a month ago. It was odd. As that last thought flickered through her mind, she drifted off with the steady roar of the wind echoing in her ears.

Alice sat up, looking out of the car into the hazy morning light, and realized she must have fallen asleep because the sun was higher. Sticky, brown shadows fell into the boxcar. Her brother was gone. She pushed her straw hat back on her forehead and frantically scanned the boxcar. A small cry rose to her lips, but died almost as it started. His brown coat caught her eye. He had his back to her talking with a group of hobos in one corner. She got up, brushing off her overalls, and walked over. Alice tapped him on the shoulder.

"Told you to stick with me, John."

"Oh, he's all right, ma'am," a young voice announced. Alice looked up to receive a huge grin from a boy with flaming red hair, freckles dotting his cheeks and dimples cutting into his dirty skin. She was startled to see someone so young, as young as she was, propped up on a tin bucket holding conference with other young hobos. John grabbed hold of her coat sleeve, his face bright.

"Alice, this is Tex—he's been all over the country—and this is Walter and Jimmy. They're Hoover Tourists!"

"That's a nice way of saying we're bums," the one called Walter chimed in. Alice smiled. The boy had thick black hair and wire-rimmed glasses, but his face, just like Tex's, was smeared with soot. She could tell by the way he carried himself, his mannerisms and his words, that he was probably smart as a whip. Walter stuck out a hand and Alice took it. Tex came next, lifting his scrawny backside off the bucket and pumping her hand twice. He made a strange clicking noise in his throat.

"Please to make your acquaintance, ma'am."

"Alice Horton," she nodded as another boy with thin brown hair stood up and shook her hand with a firm grip.

"I'm Jimmy Redland," he said, returning her nod then sitting down. His eyes were the color of smooth river rocks—gray with small flecks of blue.

Tex broke out a harmonica and brushed it on his dirty overalls. "Big John was telling us about why you had to leave home. That's a downright shame, ma'am."

"You don't have to call me 'ma'am'," Alice said. "I'm only twelve."

"Just showing respect." Tex laughed and started playing the harmonica. The random conversations in the boxcar ceased. Faces turned in the morning light to listen as Tex whipped the harmonica across his lips. Music filled the wind.

Alice eased herself down beside Jimmy and listened to Tex play "Did You Ever See a Dream Walking?" while John propped his elbows on his knees and cradled his face in his hands with wonder. Alice could tell her little brother was caught up in the adventure of all this and did not really understand that they might not see their parents for a long time—years maybe. She knew nothing of her Aunt Effigy, but she felt cautious. Something tickled at her brain and ached to be scratched. Vowing to make the best of whatever situation came along, she told herself everything would be fine. Her mother had given her only one cryptic piece of advice: "I ain't seen Effigy in years, Alice. When she came of age, she didn't want much to do with family and moved to Carson Corners. Just do what she tells you. Don't sass her and make sure John behaves himself."

"He's a show off," Jimmy said, nodding toward Tex.

Alice looked over and smiled. "He's pretty good."

"That harmonica has gotten us out of some jams."

"How long you been riding?"

"Almost a year. Walter, Tex and I were all in the Lutheran Orphanage out of Boise, Idaho. It was a pretty bad place so we started off to ride the rails and see if we could find work. Now we just go where the wind carries us. We try to get work picking whatever's in season. Not much money this year, though, and winter is coming on. Your brother said it's the first time y'all ever caught a train. Is that right?"

"Yeah. It was a little scary."

"We've been riding so long feels like we've caught a million trains. Tex knows just about everything you can imagine about the train routes, the bulls to avoid in the switchyards…you name it and he knows it."

"I do," Tex bragged, the music from his harmonica ending with an off-key whistle. "Yes, I do indeed. Walter and Jimmy are about the best buddies a guy can have. We've rode the rails together, learned the ins and outs and here we are, free as birds."

"Wow," John whispered.

"Easy, there." Walter laughed, adjusting his glasses. "It sounds glamorous, but it's not so much fun when you're starving."

"Amen to that," Jimmy joined in.

"How do you live?" Alice asked. "I mean, without any money or food?"

"Lots of ways," Tex answered, dropping his harmonica back in the top pocket of his overalls. "We scout out bakeries and sometimes they let us have doughnuts that are two or three days old. Not always fresh, but it'll fill you up. We put the bum on a restaurant."

"What's that?" John asked with large eyes. Tex cleared his throat.

"One of us will go into a diner and climb up at the counter beside some folks. We ask the waitress if she has anything she can spare 'cause we haven't eaten in days. Nine out of ten times, the person next to you will give you some of their leftovers. Or better yet they'll say, 'just put it on my tab' and you're eatin' like a king," Tex said with a big smile. "You do what you can when you're on the nut."

"Huh?" Alice asked.

"No money," Walter translated.

"Oh. It's that easy, huh?"

"Not always." Walter sighed. Tex started to jump in, hooking his thumbs through the straps of his faded overalls, ready for a speech on life as a wanderer, but Walter held up a slim hand with dirt-stained fingers. "Don't start that 'freedom of the road' malarkey, Tex. Sometimes we get thrown out of places and sometimes people will call the police. We've all ended up in jail at one time or another."

"Good food and lodgings." Jimmy shrugged.

"Yes," Walter agreed with a sigh, "but hard labor usually went with it. No matter how often you catch out, you have to always remember one mistake can be your last. If the bulls don't get you, there are always the cops and don't think the trains are safe. There was a little kid that came along a few months ago and slipped trying to hop a freighter. He dropped under the train and that was the last of him. We've seen other hobo's beaten by the bulls—dragged right out of the cars and beaten. You've got to watch the railroad bulls. We all stay clear of Texas. They are real hard on guys trying to make their own way."

"And Cheyenne, Wyoming!" Tex snarled. "They got a school where they train guys to be railroad bulls. Meaner than snakes."

"We're on our way to Carson Corners," John said, his eyes doubtful. He thought if these boys grimaced and said, *'Oh, you'll want to stay clear of that place'*, he'd talk his sister into fending for themselves on the rails. He liked these three nomads and thought bumming around the country with them at his side wouldn't be the worst thing anyone ever did.

Jimmy was laughing.

"Don't worry, you'll get there fine. We're all heading east anyway. We'll get off at Carson Corners with you just to be sure. They got a nice hobo jungle there. Might be time to take a load off."

"John was telling us about your aunt," Tex said, picking his teeth with his fingernail. "She friendly toward bo's? Give handouts?"

"I don't know." Alice shrugged. "We've never met her. We didn't know we had an aunt until about a month ago. Nobody at home ever talked about her, at least not around us."

"Mama doesn't like her," John huffed. "She said she's greedy."

"John!" Alice snapped.

"I heard her and papa talking and she said Aunt Effigy might cook us and eat us!"

"She did not." Alice turned her attention back to Walter, Tex and Jimmy. "I think there was some bad blood. Mama's never talked about it much, but I think our aunt just didn't want anything to do with our family. She sent a letter years ago saying she never wanted to see mama again. Poor mama...she said she wrote letter after letter, pleading with Aunt Effigy to explain why, but never heard a thing. After that, mama and papa just respected her wishes and stayed clear."

"At least you've got somewhere to go," Walter said with a sad smile.

"You have each other," Alice said, nodding toward the three of them.

"Wouldn't trade them for the world." Jimmy laughed.

They passed the day getting to know each other and listening to Tex play the harmonica. As the day lingered and long shadows cut across the train car, Alice wandered over by the door and sat down. She swung her feet out into the cold wind and gripped the side of the metal frame for support. The world rushed by, but she could pick out a few stray stars over the hills. Alice glanced back and found John curled up asleep next to Tex and Walter. Tex had his head back and his mouth open, snoring louder than the rumbling of the tracks. She could hear him from where she sat. Walter slumped in one corner, his glasses hanging off the edge of his thin nose. Jimmy got up and joined her near the car door.

"You might want to bring your feet in," he said, dropping down next to her and inching his back against the freight door.

"Why?"

"If we cross a bridge, the tresses will catch your foot and drag you over. I've seen it happen more than once."

"Oh," Alice said, whipping her legs back inside the car and swallowing the lump that rose in her throat. She changed the subject. "How old are you?"

"Thirteen. So is Walter. Tex is twelve."

"You like living on the rails?" she asked.

"It's all right. Get to go all over the country and meet lots of folks. We've done fruit harvesting in California and ridden the top of boxcars running across the Great Plains or hunkered down on the blinds of the Twentieth Century Limited. Course, we almost froze to death once or twice riding the blinds of a Super Chief. And hot cinders can get into your lungs and you'll spit blood for days."

15

Alice grimaced, but Jimmy shrugged.

"It's not so bad. We got our stuff in a bindle, all we would ever need, we bum food whenever we can and sometimes we eat, sometimes we don't. We've seen the big hobo jungles in Sandusky, Ohio and Pocatello, Idaho. We've been chased outta towns and train yards from San Francisco to Boston and back."

"Sounds kind of dangerous, Jimmy."

"You just gotta look before you leap. We should be in North Carolina tomorrow and we'll help y'all get off the train. There's a big 'bo jungle there in Carson Corners. If you want to join us, I'm sure we can find some chicory and dirt, heat a little water and make coffee. You're welcome to share."

"Thanks." She smiled and reached into her pocket, pulling out the food her mother had given her. She gave some to Jimmy and nibbled on some dried beef. "Give some to Walter and Tex when they wake up. I saved some for John."

"We appreciate it." He smiled back. All night, whenever Alice woke up on the floor of the train car, she saw Jimmy nearby. At first she thought he was asleep, even though he was sitting up with his head back against the car, but then, in a patch of cold moonlight, she saw that his eyes were open.

"You awake?" she whispered. He nodded and leaned over, his face black in the darkness. She could just make out his thin, handsome features.

"Keeping watch. It ain't always safe for a girl to travel on the rails. Just want to make sure nobody tried to mess with you in the night."

Alice said nothing, but she settled back down across her forearm, smelling her father's scent in the old coat, a familiar smell of aftershave and sweat. She smiled in the dark, glad to have Jimmy awake and watching out for them.

——

"Get ready," Jimmy yelled and Alice gripped John's hand tighter than she meant to. Her nails dug into his skin.

"Ouch," he moaned, ripping his hand away. "Sweet Little Orphan Annie, that hurts."

"Sorry."

The train slowed down as the midmorning sun blazed in the cold October sky. Tex had his hat stuffed on his head and a bit of Bull Durham tobacco in his mouth. A huge lopsided smile stretched from ear to ear across his face. Walter looked like he was facing a firing squad. Jimmy leaned closer to Alice and John and shouted over the train's whistle.

"Remember to hit the ground running or you'll fall!"

Tex threw back his head and laughed. "Don't hit a rock or signal standard, neither."

And, as quick as lighting, Tex was gone. He leaped from the doorway in a blur of color and landed in the dry weeds along the tracks, running. They saw him whip his hat off and wave to them as the train continued down the tracks.

"I've always hated this part," Walter complained and then jumped.

"Okay," Jimmy said, inching closer to the door. "This is it. We gotta jump."

"This is so cool," John said under his breath. Before

Jimmy or Alice could stop him, he was out the door, leaping into a pile of weeds and puddles, running and shouting.

"Brave little kid," Jimmy said with a smile.

"He's a nut. Okay, let's get this over with." Alice put the toes of her boots against the edge of the train car. In the distance she could see the dense pine trees shadowing the land and a thin layer of mist hovering above the fields in the sunlight. Jimmy took her hand and they looked at each other. The cars were slowing and the train yard was not far off as they both flung their bodies from the doorway. Alice clamped her eyes shut and fell into darkness. The next thing she knew Walter, Tex, Jimmy and her little brother hovered over her.

"You okay?" John asked, patting her head.

"What happened?" She was stretched out in the dirt, cold blades of grass under her back. The few stray freckles dotted across her nose made a sharp contrast with her pale face in the clear morning light.

"You took quite a tumble, missy. It was pretty as a train wreck." Tex snorted and Walter elbowed him in the gut, knocking the wind from his laughter. John helped his sister up and Jimmy picked up her straw hat, handing it back to her.

"Not bad for a first jump."

"I feel like I've been hit by a tornado."

"Happens all the time," Walter said. "First time we jumped, Tex landed in a patch of cow manure."

"Shut up!" Tex snapped.

"C'mon," Jimmy said, and the five of them collected their bindles and stared down the dusty stretch of road. The top of a steeple peeked through a cluster of pine and oak trees way off in the distance. Toward the far left of the train yard they saw the shantytowns in a large field. There were wooden shacks and barrels with small fires burning and a clear stream running alongside the tracks.

"The jungle?" Alice asked.

"That's it," Walter said. "We'll go in and meet the old hobo buzzard that's made himself king. We'll have to hit the stem and see what we can find in the way of food."

"That's the way it works," Jimmy said with a wink toward Alice. "We have to bring something to the jungle, food or money or something. Everyone pitches in and brings whatever they can rustle up. Tonight the whole camp will be dining on Mulligan Stew."

"Thanks for the food, you guys," Walter said and clamped a hand on John's shoulder. "It helped keep the hunger pains away this morning. Now, you stay with your sister, John. Do what she tells you, okay?"

"Yes, sir!" John snapped to attention. Alice was amazed at the amount of respect her brother showed these boys.

"Alice, it was very nice to meet you," Walter continued with a small bow that, coming from him, seemed simple and natural rather than ridiculously formal and out of place. She smiled and nodded.

"See ya', kids," Tex said.

Jimmy shrugged his shoulders. "Well, I'm sure we'll be hanging out here for a day or two and then it's back to catching out. Take care and don't let that aunt of yours spoil you too much. If we're back through this way, we might look you up."

"We'd be mighty proud if you did," Alice smiled. "We'll be staying with Effigy Goode. We don't know where she lives, but her store is on Main Street. Drop by anytime. You're always welcome."

"Bye," John said with a small wave, as Alice and John started down the dirt road. They both craned their heads to look back inside the hobo jungle at the makeshift metal and wood buildings and the curls of smoke drifting from the fires into the sky. Their three friends vanished among the other people roaming by the tracks.

Chapter Two

Meeting Aunt Effigy — Yuck, Ugh & Triple Phooey

"Well, this ain't what I expected. It's kinda nice." John gawked as they entered the town limits and saw the stores along Main Street. It was a bustling little town with a courthouse surrounded by thin, barren trees. A clock on the top of the white courthouse proclaimed it almost eleven. A Model T Ford rattled down the street blasting its horn while men and women moved down the sidewalks. A bakery on the corner forced Alice and John to press their faces against the glass and stare inside at the warm rolls and freshly baked bread. They had stuffed down the last of the food while on the train and, after sharing what they had with Jimmy, Tex and Walter, there had been precious little food left. The smells from the bakery made them lick their lips.

"Do you hear that?" she asked.

"What?"

"Is that my stomach growling or a panther behind us?"

John smiled and pushed Alice, both of them running down the street, the soles of their old boots flopping against the sidewalk.

"You think Aunt Effigy will feed us?"

"I hope so."

"Where do we find her?"

"Mama said it was the largest store on Main Street and we couldn't miss it. She said..." Alice's voice died into silence.

"What?" John asked, glancing up at Alice's face. He followed her gaze and the two of them stood staring down the street in silence. Filling up an entire corner of the block, stood an old, brick building, two stories tall with windows looking out into the street. Bright, red letters filled the sign above the glass windows and read:

GOODE'S MERCANTILE

"Well, I'll be an A&P Gypsy," John whispered.

"I second that."

"Let's go!" John shouted. They ran across the street, dodged a few black cars and slid to a stop. The sunlight reflected off the windows, making it impossible for either one of them to see inside. All they could see in the glare were two thin children in heavy clothing—their own reflections. Alice grabbed a handful of her brother's coat and dragged him with her through the doors into the warm interior. The walls were brick, but lined with electric lights. They had funnel-shaped metal covers that pooled circles of yellow light along the wooden floors. The store was filled with a hushed silence, almost a kind of reverence, like in a library or a church. All around John and Alice, the people inside the store moved like ghosts, sorting through the dry goods and clothes. They were only darkly dressed shapes drifting in slow, hazy motions. In the middle of the store, a long wooden staircase led to a second level with a metal balcony. Offices lined the upper part of the store and frosted glass windows set in the doors occasionally displayed a shadowy figure moving back and forth behind the glass. Alice heard her brother's voice loud and clear from somewhere to her right.

"Can you get my Aunt Effigy? Tell her that family's come calling."

Alice glanced over and saw him talking to a woman in a polka dot print dress with a white lace collar. Alice rushed over and put her arm around John's shoulder.

"I'm sorry, ma'am, he's a little excited. We just got into town. Can you tell us where we'd find Miss Goode?"

The woman wrinkled her pretty face. Her tongue slipped into the side of her cheek making a bulge. She stood like that for a few moments, frozen in thought, and then blinked rapidly breaking the spell. Her deep red hair—the color made Alice think of firelight—was tied back from her face. "You're related to Miss Goode?"

"Yep," John said nodding. "I'm her nephew."

"I didn't know she had any family." The woman looked bewildered. "Gosh, well, she's upstairs right now, in her office. You stay right here and I'll see if I can find somebody to…to tell her you're here. Maybe I'll just go up there. Yes, that's what I'll do. Now, don't go anywhere, okay?"

Alice and John nodded in unison as the woman walked away in a hurry, her shoes making tiny clicks on the wooden floor. John bolted around a table of work pants with Alice on his heels, snagging the back of his coat.

"No, you don't. You're not going anywhere."

"I just wanna look around," John whined. Alice shook her head.

"No. That lady told us to stay put, so put we'll stay."

Alice inched John in front of her and wrapped her arms around his shoulders. They stepped back out of the way for a few customers. John's feet were getting itchier by the second, but Alice held tight, shifting her eyes around her. The store was bigger than she had expected. *Maybe we'll be able to help out some,* she thought. *We could earn a little money and send some back to mama and papa. I bet this store is nice in the winter. It feels so warm and the lights are kinda low. Makes me a little sleepy,* she thought.

"Here she comes," John whispered. The same woman they had met was coming down the long flight of steps, wringing her hands together. She bit her lower lip as she approached them.

"I'm Anne," the woman said, her voice coming out in a gust of air while her fragile smile brightened her face. "You're John and Alice, right?"

"That's us!" John said.

"Climb those stairs, take a right, and it's the big door at the end of the hallway."

"Really?" Alice asked and felt a huge sense of relief when the woman nodded and cast her eyes upward toward the second landing.

"She said she wanted both of you in her office immediately."

"Thanks, ma'am," Alice said and she and John started through the store. Anne called them back, her voice diving into a soft whisper. She played with the gold chain at her throat and glanced around to see if anyone was listening.

"Children, do you know your aunt...very well?"

"No, never met her," Alice said.

"Well, she's temperamental," Anne said with a nervous laugh.

"What's that mean?" John asked.

"It means," Alice said, "she gets ornery."

"Exactly," Anne said, rolling her eyes and letting out a heavy breath. "You don't need to be frightened. Just listen to what she says, don't interrupt and you'll do fine."

Alice and John walked to the base of the stairs and looked up into the shadowy second floor. Each of them cast a glance at the other and then started up the stairs. Alice noticed how their footsteps caused a slight echo on the wooden stairs. When they reached the second landing, her hand touched the cold, metal railing. She looked over the balcony. The tables and shelves, which seemed like an endless maze down on the floor, were clearly defined from up here. She scanned the store for a moment, seeing Anne's pale face still watching them from the dry goods section. Her red hair stood out like a candle flame in the shadows. Alice waved and Anne waved back feebly. John squeezed Alice's hand and they walked down the long shadowy corridor, approaching the double doors at the end. A small brass plate was attached to the door:

E. Goode, Owner

Alice rapped her knuckles against the door and waited. There was no sound. She knocked again, louder this time. She looked at John. Dark shadows of soot had been embedded in the grooves of his face and she wished she had a little water to clean him up before going in. A horrible thought occurred to her. If John were covered in soot, she was probably coated too. She removed her hat and tried to smooth down her brown hair. She pulled tiny bits of grass from her pigtails.

Before she realized it, John had turned the knob. The door opened into a large office with burgundy velvet drapes framing the windows that looked out onto Main Street. Streams of sunlight slanted through the windows while tiny motes swam in the light, dancing down to the thick, dark brown rug. A mahogany desk, that seemed almost as big as the freight car that brought them to Carson Corners, sat in front of one wall. It was a massive piece with carved fleur-de-lis and wild pheasants taking flight from grassy fields carved along the front of the desk.

"Come in," a voice shouted and they both jumped over the threshold into the room. From the top of the desk peered a pale face framed by black hair tied into a bun. The owner of the face snapped her fingers and pointed to a spot just in front of the desk. Alice and John hurried forward. A huge Great Dane padded on thick paws around the desk and stared at them, growling softly.

"Down, Rufus!" the voice commanded and the Great Dane eased to the floor, his eyes ever vigilant. Alice and

John crept forward. Up close, Alice thought the pheasants carved in the desk seemed to be moving. Their wings were oiled to a bright shine and seemed to be flapping in the dim lights, flying across a sleek wooden sky. Alice swallowed hard, tasting the last bit of dried beef from this morning.

A white moon of a face slid up over the desk to look down at them from the shadowy gloom. A black eye patch darkened Effigy Goode's face and her good eye, the left one, peered out at them as black as midnight behind a pair of glasses trimmed with small diamonds. The glasses were fixed to a chain around her neck and a smile snaked across her face lined in bright red lipstick. Thin wrinkles fanned out under her eyes and around her lips, but the rest of the face was doused in pale makeup.

"Ma'am," Alice said and felt silly doing it, but she curtsied before she could stop herself. "I'm Alice Hor—"

"I know who you are," the cold voice croaked. "You're Alice and this is John."

The black eye slid over. Alice knew that if she had not been holding her brother by the arm he would have taken a step backward. He tried, but she held firm, anchoring him in place. He kind of rocked on his heels and stared with wide eyes at the woman in front of him.

"I've had nothing to do with my sister for almost thirty years. I've made it quite clear in the past that our relationship is dead. So, she contacts me after all this time and what did she want? Not to ask how I managed on my own. Not for an explanation of how I retained a booming business in the face of overwhelming financial obstacles. Not to ask anything except that I take in the spawn of her marriage to some

~~drunken, lazy, good-for-nothing, shiftless bum you call~~ *daddy*."

Alice heard her brother gulp. It was as loud as a scream.

"I agreed to let you both come here out of the goodness of my heart. It's a misconception around this town that I don't even have a heart, but I assure you that, as an upstanding Christian woman, I am given to help the needy from time to time. So, let me show you around."

The chair slid back and Effigy Goode came around the end of the desk. She was short and thin, dressed in a smart gray wool suit with black lapels. Her thick black soles *thumped* on the floor as she marched over to the door. She twirled one hand at the end of her bony wrist, bracelets jingling like coins, and motioned them through. Alice and John slipped through the doorway as if she might bite them, followed by Rufus. Effigy Goode closed the door to her office and strolled down the hallway, stopping at a door to her left. She opened it and began descending a stairwell. John and Alice followed, hugging the wall. John leaned over until his lips touched his sister's ear. He whispered as soft as a mouse chewing through wood, "She looks like a pirate wearing that patch." Rufus gave a low snarl behind them and Alice could feel John clutching her arm. He made a soft cry in the back of his throat. "Where are we going?"

"It's okay," she whispered.

Ahead of them, Aunt Effigy appeared to be swallowed up in the blackness. It wasn't until they reached the bottom of the steps that they realized she had opened another door and had vanished into the dark interior. A bare light bulb flickered on and Alice and John were in the store cellar. It was dank and shadows floated like ghosts along the walls.

"Here you go," Effigy Goode announced with a hint of glee to her voice. Under the lone light bulb hanging from its cord, Effigy Goode's one eye was lined with thick black shadows and her face was washed stark white. Alice and John stepped into the oppressive cellar and walked down the rickety wooden stairs to the stone floor. Shelves lined the walls and boxes stacked in random order teetered in every corner. They looked like they would topple if you breathed on them.

"This is the store's cellar where we keep some of the extra inventory. All the items that remain in stock are stored down here. It's a bit dusty."

"It's...real nice." Alice shrugged.

"Over here is the boiler room." Aunt Effigy pointed a bony finger toward a small side room without a door. The children stuck their heads in and saw the massive iron boiler in the corner, humming and growling like a living animal. Flickers of firelight danced off the brick walls. A wooden container near the corner of the room acted as the coal bin. The shovel stood in the corner and a small wagon with a handle was propped near the doorway.

"You'll have to get the boiler started every morning before seven so the store will be warmed by the time we open at eight. You'll have to stoke the boiler throughout the day. There's not much to it. Open the grate, toss in the coal and keep the fire going. A trained monkey could do it. That's sort of what you'll be—trained monkeys."

John fought the urge to do his best impression of a monkey. He wanted to curl his hands under his arms and lurch around the cellar squawking and chattering, but Effigy Goode's cold stare stopped him. He sidled over to his sister. Rufus had remained sitting on the stairs, his gray ears standing up, ever alert.

"We stay down here all day?" Alice asked in a tiny voice.

"Yes...and all night. These will be your new living quarters."

"Are you bananas?" John shouted with wide eyes.

Effigy allowed that snake of a smile to inch along her lips. "It's bound to be better than tenant farming."

"But there might be spooks down here," John hissed, glancing around him as if the shadows were pressing in to swallow him whole.

"Nonsense," she snapped.

"Won't it be cold?" Alice asked.

"It'll be fine during the day because the boiler will keep it warm and there are some old blankets down here if it gets cold in the night. I'll have some of my employees bring you a plate from the diner every evening. You will have to share. Whatever the special is for the day, that's what you're getting. You'll also have a piece of fruit in the mornings. The side door leading into the alley will remain unlocked. There's an outhouse behind the store...please use it. You are never to go into the store unless given permission by myself or by one of the employees." She walked up the wooden steps toward the stairwell, pivoting on her black heels by Rufus and standing with her hands clasped in front of her. "Is that understood?"

Alice nodded. "Yes, Aunt Eff-"

"It will be *Miss Goode* to you."

Alice cast her eyes down to the slate floor. The huge

slabs of stone were smooth on the rounded edges with tiny trails of mica running through the rock causing strange reflections in the light. It looked like slug trails.

"You will have to fetch the coal from the hopper every few days to make sure we are amply supplied. They will put everything on my bill. You can use the wagon in the boiler room and walk to the train yard. Any questions?"

"What about school?"

"What about it? Were you in school in Alabama?"

"No ma'am, but only because mama and papa needed our help on the farm."

"Well, I need you here so you can put any schooling right out of your mind. Understood?"

"What if we leave?" John asked and Alice's mouth dropped open.

"John, be still!"

"What if you do?" Miss Goode asked in a soothing voice. "There's the door on the other side of the cellar. Walk up the steps, turn the knob and you'll be in the alley next to the undertakers. Be my guest."

"No, that's all right," Alice said, putting a hand on John's shoulder. She could feel his whole body tensed like one giant spring, ready to uncoil and shoot up the steps at their aunt. "We'll be just fine."

"Sensible girl. You'll have a roof over your heads and food in your stomach. That's all Eunice asked of me and that's all I'm providing. If these accommodations don't suit you, feel free to leave. I won't shed a tear."

"I bet you won't," John growled. His face was gray with rage.

Alice held him back. She had seen her brother lose his temper before. Effigy Goode chuckled. It was a vile sound like rocks being scraped together.

"You can always go back to that hovel and starve with your parents."

"You wicked old wit-"

Alice clamped a hand over her brother's mouth, cutting off his words. Rufus gave a single bark, strong and scary. Miss Goode glanced down and reached out her hand. The dog licked the back of her hand once and went quiet. Turning her attention back to John, she gave him an eerie smile.

"Careful now, my tiny monkey. That mouth will get you in trouble. We might yet have to snip out that tongue and make you a little mute. Would you like that?"

"Fire's getting low." Alice nodded toward the boiler, changing the subject. She kept one hand over John's mouth and the other snared in his clothing so he couldn't escape. "We'll get to work now, ma'am."

"There's running water from an old spigot out back and some rags and a pail. Tidy it up a bit in here and see if it doesn't get more cheery."

John tried his best to wiggle out of Alice's hands as Miss Goode fiddled with her keys. His feet slapped at the stone floor, as he tried to run. Alice held tight. She pictured his brown boots connecting with the floor and a whirl of dust flying from his feet as he burned the soles of his shoes flying up the steps and knocking Miss Goode for a loop.

"Ouch," John hissed, looking at his sister, his eyes narrowed into slits. "You're diggin' into my skin."

"Be still," Alice whispered. "That dog would swallow you in one gulp."

"This door leading up into the main portion of the building will always be locked. As you can see, there is another door just through the alcove." Effigy Goode motioned to the right and Alice could see a thin trail of light framing a door in the darkness. "This leads into the ground floor portion of the store. It will be locked as well. Oh—by the way," Miss Goode said turning with a sneer. "I don't think there are any rats down here, but you can leave the light bulb burning all night. I'll allow you that indulgence. It'll keep the roaches from running over your face in the dark. And if it slipped my mind, let me just add…welcome home." She turned with a snap of her black heels. Rufus slipped through the door with her and then the sound of a key being turned in the rusty lock echoed in the shadows. They were alone in the cellar.

"She's a piece of work," Alice mumbled.

"No wonder mama didn't talk about her. She'd give Lucifer himself a run for his money. Let's go."

"Where?"

"Home."

"It's not that bad, John. We'll fix it up and it'll be swell. You'll see."

"Let's leave," he whined tugging on her sleeve.

"We can't go back to Alabama! There's no food and no money to buy food and we'd starve before Christmas."

"Then let's hit the rails like Jimmy and Tex and Walter." Alice huffed. "No."

"We could go wherever we wanted."

"Let's just stay here awhile. We'll see what happens."

"Let's not," John pleaded. He thrust his hands on his hips. "You want to shove coal for that old bat and live in her cellar?"

"We'll clean it up."

"I'm scared," John said glancing around at the long, lazy shadows.

"It's warm." Alice laughed, trying to make the best of an awful situation. She knew it was bad, but put on the best face she could muster to cheer up her brother.

"I'm hungry."

"Here," she said, pulling out a small bit of leftover fried dough. He took it, slumping down on an upturned orange crate. Alice walked into the shadowy corners of the store's cellar and breathed a sigh. "Okay, let's stoke the boiler and see if we can't turn this place into something nice."

Chapter Three

Bob Craven
and the Cellar Sounds

(No, it's not a musical act)

Alice returned from behind the store with her sleeves rolled up, a thin line of sweat across her forehead and mud on her boots. The wooden door was propped open with a broken piece of brick. She stomped down into the cellar, toting another bucket of water with her as darkness descended on Main Street. Alice set the bucket on the floor and turned with a satisfied smile. In only a few short hours they had swept and scrubbed the floor near the boiler room, cleared out some storage areas and shoved boxes back into the far reaches of the cellar. Alice glanced around.

"John?"

The cellar looked deserted except for the mountains of boxes near the back shelves. The heat from the boiler was starting to die out as the last of the day's coal burned away.

"John, where are you?"

A soft giggle escaped the darkness. She brushed her fingers over the brick wall for support as she inched into the back part of the cellar. Her eyes grew accustomed to the darkness little by little.

"I know you're back here."

A darker shape burst from the shadows. Alice half screamed. She knew John was trying to frighten her and, even knowing it, she still had gone all goose pimply when he jumped from behind the boxes.

"I wasn't scared," she shouted and then got a good look at her littler brother. She burst out laughing. John had an old fur stole gathered around his neck. It looked like it had seen better days since most of the fur had fallen out. He wore a pale green dress that gathered in folds around his feet and a purple hat with wide red ostrich feathers swooping up from the band. Alice dropped to her knees laughing as John played with the string of fake pearls around his neck and began stomping around in a pair of high heels too big for his feet.

"My name is Effigy Goode," he shrieked in a falsetto voice. "That's *Miss Goode* to you, ragamuffin! I want y'all to clean my dirty cellar and keep that boiler going so no one upstairs gets cold. Laws a mercy, I can't have nobody gettin' cold in my store. Are you listenin' to me, little monkey?"

"Yes, ma'am," Alice managed to mutter through her laughter. "Where did you find that stuff?"

"There's a bunch of old clothes marked as trash. Boxes full of 'em." He giggled.

"Halloween's a few weeks off, but you look great. I wish

mama could see you."

"I was thinking we should take some of the clothes and stuff them inside other clothes and make some bedding."

"Good idea."

"And the rest of the stuff we could take down to the hobo town and give to Walter, Tex and Jimmy."

"They would never look that good in dresses."

"Stop it," he chuckled, taking the hat off his thin, blond hair. He tossed it in the corner. "There's a whole bunch of stuff—coats, pants, shirts. Most of it's too big for them, but some of it would be real keen."

"We've got to get coal tomorrow. We'll bundle some of it together and take it down. If they've hopped another train, we'll leave the clothes in the hobo jungle. Maybe someone can use them."

"You think they've left?"

"I don't know," she shrugged.

"If they're still around, why don't we go with them?"

"Don't start that again."

"We don't-"

Alice held up a finger to her lips and shifted her eyes to the right. John listened as well and heard someone tapping at the door to the alley.

"Hello?" a voice called.

"Get those things off," Alice hissed and ran back to the front of the cellar. As she rounded the corner of the stairs she saw a tall, lanky figure moving down inside. "Who are you?"

"Well, hello there. I hope I'm not interrupting."

As the man reached the bottom of the steps, she could see he had a full head of white hair swept back from his forehead. He was thin, almost too thin, and wore a dark blue suit and a red muffler wrapped around his neck. A big smile slipped over his wrinkled face and two bright blue eyes peered from inside wire spectacles.

"Hi," Alice muttered.

"I brought you a plate from the diner down the street," he said holding out a cloth-covered dish. Alice heard John's footsteps as he came running out of the dark. Both children seized the plate from the stranger's grip and crouched to the floor. They ripped the cloth away and began eating so fast the man plopped down on the bottom slab of the step with a gasp.

"You must be starved!"

John mumbled between gulping a bite of food and taking another hunk off the drumstick. He twirled a hand out in front of him in an exaggerated pantomime as if this indicated all the stranger would ever need to know, while incomprehensible grunts escaped his bulging jaws. Before catching a breath, he shoveled another pile of carrots in his mouth using his hand as a spoon.

"Good Lord, you poor children. I'm Miss Goode's accountant, Robert Craven. I make sure everything tallies up at the end of the day, so to speak. She asked me to bring a plate down here on my way home this evening. I think she asked because I was the only one still around. Seems like I'm always working late, you know?"

"You talk funny," Alice said, stuffing a biscuit in her mouth in one gigantic bite. "'Rooufrmarondtesearts?"

"I beg your pardon, lass?"

"I said 'are you from around these parts'?"

"Oh, no...not originally. I was born in London. I was apprenticed there before coming here and working for Miss Goode. You know, she didn't tell me anything about you. I was just instructed to fetch a plate for two orphaned children she said were living down here."

"We're not orphans," Alice said, rolling her eyes. "We're her niece and nephew."

"You're sporting with me now?"

"Nah," John grunted with another handful of food crammed in his mouth.

"So, Miss Goode is your *aunt?*"

"You got it," John nodded.

"I should have known there was something odd when she said she was *graciously* allowing two destitute orphans to stay down here. She's never gracious about anything, even spit and twaddle. I'm sorry, that was rather rude of me."

Alice sat back with a tired smile. "She's making us live in her coal cellar. You can say whatever you want about her, mister."

"Oh, please—call me Bob, all right? How did you get here?"

Alice started relating the story while John continued eating. By the time she finished Bob Craven was staring at them with his bright blue eyes twinkling. "It's remarkable. You just hopped on a train and here you are. How are you two going to survive the coming winter?"

"We'll manage," Alice said but he saw the doubt in her eyes. "If we'd stayed with mama and papa, we'd be a heck of a lot hungrier than we are right now."

"Well, I'll fix the numbers a little, rearrange some of the

inventory sheets and get you some oil lamps and candles down here."

"Thanks, mister. You're a very nice man."

"Call me Bob," he insisted. "I almost forgot—I picked these up at the diner. I couldn't tack them onto Miss Goode's account because she might be looking for something like this and I'd never hear the end of it. Got these for you myself."

Bob removed some Tootsie Rolls and licorice sticks from his pockets. Alice and John stared at him with dazed expressions.

"Well, I know it's not much, just a couple coppers' worth. Go on, you can take them. Don't you like candy?"

John reached out and curled his fingers around a licorice stick. When he pulled it close to his face in the shadows, Bob could see tears in his eyes. Alice slipped a hand around her brother's shoulder with a smile.

"It's just been awhile since we've had sweets. A long time."

"I see," Bob whispered. "Well, here you go. Enjoy."

He handed all the candy over to Alice and stood up, brushing off his pants. Removing a large gold pocket watch from his vest, he checked the time. "You're very polite children and you deserve far better than this awful place. I wish you could stay with me, but there's only the one room. If you need me though, you go down Main Street, take a right on Union and I'm at Mrs. Cobbit's Boarding House. That's where a lot of the staff lives. We get room and board at a discount. I'm on the second floor, number three. All right?"

"Thank you," Alice nodded and Bob walked up the steps.

"If there's a way for you to secure the door down there, I'd suggest doing it."

"Yes, sir, there's a bolt."

"Good. We're close to the railroad and sometimes men riding the rails come into town looking for a place to sleep. Mostly harmless, but I wouldn't want them to bother you. Keep it locked until morning. I'll see you again tomorrow."

"'Night," John shouted and Bob waved, knocking the brick away and closing the wooden door behind him. "Boy, I sure do like him," John announced, sticking the licorice stick in his mouth with a smile.

"Me too. How 'bout we get some of the clothes you found and make a bed?"

Both children moved into the back of the cellar and carried big armfuls of clothes to the front where the light bulb swayed in the cold wind that crept through the chinks. Alice stuffed some clothes in the walls where large chunks of brick were missing. They sang songs while arranging clothes for their beds. When they finally stretched out, sucking on Tootsie Rolls, both of them grew silent. Alice stared at the beams in the ceiling and glanced over to say something to John, but his eyes were closed. A blustery wind crept by the building and the rattling sounds of a car could be heard on Main Street. She curled up in a ball and breathed in the dusty smell of the cellar.

———

Effigy Goode slipped on a pair of black Oriental silk slippers with delicate beading across the toes and walked to the third floor of her house. She had tied the silk sash of her green and black robe snug against her pink nightgown and carried a candle in a silver holder. The flame twisted and squirmed in the air. Entering the top of the house in silence, she sat the candle down on a small pine table and opened the French doors. She stepped out onto the widow's walk in the cold October night. Miss Goode looked into her telescope and found the dim lights along Main Street. Shadows drifted around the streets and she could see the roof of her store.

It was a mistake to let the children come, she knew that instinctively, but when the letter had arrived from Eunice Horton begging her to take in the children, she couldn't refuse. After all, that might have led to questions or the blasted mother showing up on her doorstep with her brood in tow and that just wouldn't do. No, she had done the right thing by allowing them to arrive safe and sound in Carson Corners. Anne had seen them and Robert Craven had taken them a plate. The children had been seen and that was the important part. Now there was the pickle of a problem of getting rid of them. She needed to do it without a lot of fuss or fanfare. The little one, John, was a brat and she relished the idea of taking care of him once and for all. She could tell Alice was a good worker and at least she had some manners. The girl was pretty, though—maybe *too* pretty. She had experienced her fill of pretty girls in pigtails who interfered with her plans. If they vanished, she would fall under suspicion, but probably only from the parents. The police in town kept their distance from her and, after all, she was a fine, upstanding citizen and couldn't be held responsible if two children didn't approve of the living accommodations she provided and ran away. That's the story she would stick to. If the parents showed up and made a scene, she had ways of making them vanish as well.

Her robe billowed in the wind. Miss Goode allowed herself to smile. She would give them a month to see how things worked out. If the two children proved to be decent laborers and kept the boiler going then she would keep them for awhile. If not....

A soft whine echoed from the room behind her. Miss Goode snapped her head around and saw Rufus standing in the doorway. She walked over and scratched behind his ears.

"That's right," she sang out loud. "I have ways of disposing of little problems. If they sass me just once then I'll send them somewhere...most unpleasant."

<hr>

John awoke, his mind coming out of the darkness of sleep. He looked around and Alice was missing. Panic flooded his whole body.

"ALICE!" he yelled, leaping from the floor.

"Shhhhhhhh," she whispered from the darkness and he crept on all fours toward her voice. His heart was still hammering in his chest when he found her in the back of the cellar in almost total darkness.

"Whatcha doin'?"

"C'mere," she whispered and he sat down on the cold stone floor.

"You scared me half to death."

"Listen," she hissed.

"For what?"

"Just listen."

John sat still for a few long moments, listening to the wind outside and his breathing echoing in his ears. And then, he heard soft, muted laughter. Wrinkling his eyebrows he leaned closer to the floor. *It must be my imagination,* he thought. It happened again. John scooted back and looked at his sister's dark shape in front of him.

"It's spooks!"

"I don't think so," Alice said. "I tracked it over here. I've heard seagulls and people whispering and wolves howling and laughter and shouting and foghorns."

"*Busy* spooks."

"There's no such thing as ghosts," she snapped. "It almost sounds like a radio that's turned on somewhere."

"You think?" John asked, brightening.

"I don't know. Maybe it's upstairs. We could be hearing it through the vents, but it almost sounds like it's coming from under the floor."

"There might be an old Crosley or Zenith buried down here!"

"It wouldn't be able to pick up reception if it was buried in the floor or in the walls. Would it?"

"I dunno," John muttered with the idea sinking in. "Maybe you're right, it's upstairs and we're just hearing the echo. Wow, wouldn't it be cool to be able to listen to *Jack Benny* or *Chandu the Magician? Charlie Chan!*"

"Hold your horses," Alice said, standing up and walking back to the bedding with John hopping around behind her. "We don't even know if it *is* a radio."

"We could hear *The Lone Ranger, Lum & Abner, Dick Tracy!*"

"Let's get some sleep," she said, flopping back into the clothes. It was almost an hour later before John stopped running through his favorite radio programs and drifted off. Even then, he continued to mumble in his sleep. Alice was exhausted and closed her eyes, still listening to the faint whispers coming from the far side of the cellar. Once or twice she opened one eye and stared into the black corners and wished she could make out what was being said, but it was too faint. Those distant voices were gone when they woke up.

—

"C'mon," John shouted as they made their way down the road toward the tracks. As they cleared the town limits, a huge freight train was just pulling out of the yard, the black coils of smoke boiling into the sky. Walking alongside the dirt road, Alice and John each had a snug grip on the wagon's handle. The wind was cold. The leaves were changing colors and some of the dead ones floated by their feet and then swirled off into the fields.

"I see the Hoovervilles," Alice said and their pace quickened. The wagon was overflowing with clothes they had salvaged from the cellar of *Goode's Mercantile*. As they cleared the trees, they could see the shantytowns scattered around the open field.

"Boy, I hope the fellas are still here," John said.

They dragged the wagon into the maze of ramshackle houses. Barrels of burning scrap wood gave off gray curls of smoke and ragged men sat outside the wood and metal houses. A few men nodded and smiled, others kept their faces down, staring at the dirt and grass with faraway looks in their eyes. Children ran around, kicking an old tin can. John stopped and asked an old hobo with a dark suit and tie if he knew Walter, Tex or Jimmy, but he said he didn't. Next, they asked a group of hobos standing around a metal trash can where a fire licked at the inside and peeked over the edges.

"We've got at least one hundred folks around here, men, women, children. Ask Old Willie," one of the men grunted and pointed down a small patch of grass to a wooden shack with newspapers stuffed in the cracks to keep out the cold. "He's the buzzard that runs this place."

"Thinks he does," one of the men countered and they all laughed.

"You gonna use all those coats?" another man asked. Alice and John told the group of men to pick out whatever they wanted from the wagon. The hobos dived into the folds and pulled out several pairs of shirts, pants and coats.

"Thank y'all," a man said as they dragged the wagon down the path and stopped at the wooden shack belonging to Old Willie. As if there were any doubt, a broken board had been tacked to the outside. Scribbled in dark letters were the words: *Old Willie, King of the Hobos.* Alice pounded her fist against the side and took a quick breath when the door opened and a huge man with a graying beard and piercing eyes stepped out. He was as wide as he was tall. His belt was a rope secured through the loops of his enormous gray pants. A thick winter coat, tattered at the sleeves, hung over his giant frame.

"Well, what have we here? More 'bo's just get in? Oh, no,

I see your wagon. Are you from the Sallie?"

"Huh?" Alice asked and Willie laughed. His voice was big and strong, the sound of it scattering birds from the tree-tops.

"Salvation Army? They come around sometimes, but, no, you two don't look like Sallies. Mission folk?"

"No, sir," Alice answered. "We were told you could help us. We're looking for some friends of ours."

"Nothing's free in this world, little girl...'cept riding the rails. Whatcha got to offer me in exchange?"

"Well, sir, you can have any of the clothes in here that fit you," John said.

"Let's have a look," Old Willie said and he picked through with nimble fingers stained black from soot. "Nice pair of pants here, but it ain't my size. Good strong benny, better than this one with the holes at the sleeves. Even some socks! Well, I'll be. Okay, you two, I'll take these here things, the socks and the overcoat. Welcome to the Hobo Hotel! How can we Knights of the Rail be of assistance?"

Alice and John explained who they were looking for and Old Willie sat down outside the door to his shack with a hearty laugh.

"Of course I know the boys you mean! They held up last night in an old one-eyed bandit just over the ridge. They were catching out today. Not sure if they're still around the jungle or not."

"How would we find them?" Alice asked.

Willie pointed toward the tracks. "Cross over yonder and see if you don't spot the car. It's a big one off in the weeds. If you missed 'em, scratch a message on the inside of the car and when they get back this way, they'll be bound to see it. They always snooze in that rotting car off to the side."

"Thank you, sir," Alice said and Willie laughed again.

"Sir? Haven't heard that in a while, not from the crackers around this joint. You call me Old Willie, check?"

"Thank you. Where can we get coal for Miss Goode's store in town?"

"Blackjacks are over there. You can fill your cart to the top." Willie chuckled as Alice and John started down a small hill of grass and tall weeds. They lifted the wagon over the tracks and rounded a small clearing where several abandoned train cars sat baking in the sun.

"There it is," John called and started running. He skidded to a stop in the gravel and hoisted himself up on the metal stirrup. The redline boxcar was empty. John slid down with a disappointed face. He turned his head, one eye squinted against the sunlight. "They're gone. Guess they headed out early."

"Sorry, John. I wanted to see them too."

A voice appeared out of nowhere. "What are y'all doing?"

Alice and John glanced up and saw Tex's red hair and coal-stained face hanging over the top of the car. He waved.

"Tex!" John yelled and climbed the ladder with Alice following. They mounted the top of the metal car and Alice was surprised by how far she could see from such a lofty vantage point. Tex sat up and gave John a hardy handshake. He saluted Alice by tipping a finger to his forehead and grinned a big, toothy smile.

"Taking my morning catnap. Didn't think to be seeing you two again so soon."

John dropped to his knees and began relating everything that had happened. Alice stood in the cold wind for a moment and then sat down. When John had finished, Tex let a long whistle escape his lips. "Sounds like that aunt of yours is a piece of work. You two get to thinkin' it'd be easier on the rails, you can hang with us."

"Gosh, yeah!" John shouted and then caught his sister's stern face. "Or maybe not."

"Where are Jimmy and Walter?" Alice asked.

"Went into town to see about some grub. Or work. They should be back later. Want to hang out here?"

"Can we?" John pleaded.

"No, we've got to get the coal back and make sure the boiler stays strong all day."

"Why don't you guys come to the store?" John asked. Alice started to say no and then reconsidered. No one was around after five or six in the afternoon. Bob Craven would be bringing supper after he finished work and the guys could stay with them down in the basement, as long as they were out before the store opened in the morning. The memory of the sounds echoing through the cellar the night before lingered. She felt a chill slide through her body with the thought of it. She nodded.

"Yeah, why don't you guys come down tonight, anytime after six or seven? It's 318 Main Street. There's a door in the alley between the store and the undertaker's place."

"We'll be there," Tex said with a nod. "Starvin' or stuffed as field ticks, we'll be there."

Chapter Four

Under the Slab of Stone

The remainder of the day Alice and John spent stoking the furnace and keeping the store heated. The inside of the cellar became overwhelmingly hot. Sweat rolled off their faces and drenched their clothes. Alice propped open the door leading into the alley to let in some cool October air. John continued cleaning out the cellar while Alice watched the boiler. Sounds moved above them throughout the day. They heard brief snippets of conversation, shoes moving over the floor, creaks in the wood and the general sounds from Main Street floating down the alley.

Later, the store closed and the cellar fell into silence. Alice continued to feed the boiler more coal to keep it warm as the sky deepened a dark blue. She knew they would be in for another cold night and wanted to have as much warmth as possible. Alice and John waved good night to Bob after he had brought them a plate, then got ready for the fellas to arrive. They both nibbled at their food so there would be enough to share. Bob had brought oil lamps and candles as he promised. The cellar was alive with flickering lights throwing long, wispy shadows around the walls. Alice and John went out to the back of the store. The anthracite coal left their fingers black and got into their hair and smudged their faces. When they washed off at the spigot, dark puddles of soot formed at their feet. The night was already getting colder as Alice and John hurried back downstairs and changed clothes. A little after seven, they heard tapping at the alley door. It sounded like a secret knock; two sharp raps, a pause, three short ones. Alice hopped up the steps and flipped the bolt back. Three shadows stood in the dark alley and she broke into a wide smile when Tex, Walter and Jimmy stepped into the warm, creamy candlelight.

"Howdy!" Tex shouted. Walter and Jimmy both punched him in the arm.

"Shhhhh, keep your voice down, songbird," Jimmy chuckled, closing the door behind him. John flew up the steps and saluted the guys.

"Howdy, Big John," Walter said, ruffling John's hair as he walked down the steps, adjusting his glasses.

"It sure is good to see you fellas again," John sighed as they all reached the bottom of the steps.

"Hey, Alice," Jimmy mumbled. She smiled.

"I think you two are getting sweet on each other," Tex said with his big crooked smile running along his tanned face. Jimmy rolled his eyes.

"It's not that bad down here," Walter announced, looking around. "When Tex told us you two were living in a coal cellar, we figured on the worst. It's kinda nice down here. At least you've got your own room."

"Yep...a dark, dank, smelly room," Tex muttered. Walter and Jimmy both shot him hard looks. "Sorry, you guys," Tex apologized glancing over at Alice and John. "It's nice. Real warm."

"It gets colder in the night," Alice said. "If we could keep the boiler going, it'd be fine, but Miss Goode's keen on buying only as much coal as necessary."

"We saved some grub for ya'." John ran over and pulled back a dishtowel covering the plate of pork ribs.

"Thanks!" Jimmy said with admiration. "We scored some pie earlier today and saved a piece for you two."

Walter pulled out a small homemade sack and handed it over while rubbing his thin stomach through his faded blue shirt. "Haven't had ribs in forever."

"You two are all right!" Tex laughed and all of them sat down on the floor. Walter, Tex and Jimmy started munching on the food from the diner while John and Alice each had a large helping of boysenberry pie. When he finished, John wiped his mouth on the sleeve of his shirt and announced he'd give a grand tour. With a flourish, he indicated the boiler room.

"Well, this here is where me and sis work on keeping everybody up top nice and warm. Alice helps a little, but I do most of the real work."

"Liar!" Alice laughed.

Walter chuckled too. "Some of that coal must be bigger than you, John."

"Over here," John continued while chuckling, "This is our bedding. We stuffed old clothes to make it soft."

Alice jumped up and joined him, pointing toward the

back of the cellar. "And we also have the east wing of the manor. The dining room seats fifty, we have ten bedrooms and an indoor tennis court. I spend most of my days arranging flowers since I am a lady of leisure."

"And that's the haunted section," John said, making a sucking sound with his lips. He walked over and stood on the cold slab of flooring where they heard voices the previous night. "We don't go over here much."

Walter shoved his glasses back up his nose when they started to slide. "It's been proven by scientists all over the world that the paranormal does not exist. ESP, ghosts, things of that sort just don't exist."

Jimmy looked at Alice and John. "He's our genius. Reads all the time. He even finished fourth grade."

"Well," Alice said, "I don't know if it's haunted or not, but there's something strange going on."

She related the story while John jumped in with tales of his bravery in the face of such strange occurrences.

"Ya'll belong in a nuttery," Tex said, gnawing on a rib bone.

"Tex," Jimmy groaned, "we're gonna have to sew your mouth shut."

Walter piped in. "And fill the empty space between his ears."

"I don't mean offense. John and Alice know I don't mean they really should go live in the nuthouse, but c'mon...voices in the coal cellar? Sounds like a story you'd tell sitting around the campfire."

"But we heard the sounds," John pleaded.

"He's right," Alice said. "We both heard it and this morning it was gone. It's quiet at night when the furnace isn't going and there's no one moving around upstairs and that's when you can really hear it. Tonight we'll see if it happens again."

"Tell you what," Jimmy began, "why don't we stay here with y'all? We ain't got nothing better to do than walk back to the train yard in the cold and sleep in that boxcar. We can stay down here and see if we hear anything."

"That'd be great!" John yelled. "You will? Really?"

"Sure thing."

"We'll have to be out by morning," Walter reminded them. "We have to be moving long before the sun's up or someone might see us. We'd get arrested for sure. They would think we were breaking into the store."

"No worries," Alice laughed. "There's a rooster a couple miles down the road on somebody's farm. He woke us bright and early this morning, way before light."

"You guys been up there?" Tex asked, casting his eyes toward the ceiling.

"Just once," Alice shrugged. "Yesterday. It was when we first met our aunt."

"That door over yonder? Where does it go?"

"Well, there's a stairwell that leads into the upper part where all the offices are located. There's another door just beyond that one leading into the ground floor level of the store."

"Locked, huh?" Tex asked with a mischievous gleam in his eye. "Betcha I could pick it."

"No. No way. Forget it," Walter snapped. "You'll get us all in trouble."

"He's right," Jimmy said. "Police are always up and down

the stem at night. Any lights inside and we'd be caught for sure."

"If that old witch found us up there, she'd kill us and bury us out back," Alice grumbled.

"Wouldn't have to know it was you. The three of us could go upstairs and if we got caught-"

"No," Jimmy said and his face had gone rigid. Tex pursed his lips for a few moments and then shrugged.

"Fine, have it your way. Just thought some canned food, a new belt, stuff like that would be nice."

Jimmy turned to Alice with a sigh. "Where can we bed down?"

"Anywhere you want," Alice said and they all flopped out on the stuffed clothes, giggling. After blowing out the candles, Walter showed John shadow puppets with his fingers in the glow of the one remaining oil lamp. Rabbits and dogs and bears flickered across the beams in the ceiling. Tex fell asleep before anyone else, snoring. Alice drifted off while Jimmy was telling her about the time they escaped from a group of bulls in a Georgia train yard.

When Alice woke up, the oil lamp was turned up high. Everyone was awake and huddled in the back of the cellar. Alice crawled out of the bedding and made her way over. She knew as soon as she reached them that they had heard the sounds. In fact, she could hear them too: wind, giggling, distant gunfire, barking dogs.

"What do you think?" Jimmy asked, looking over at Walter.

"We thought it might be a radio," John volunteered, but Walter shook his head.

"Nope, couldn't be a radio. It sounds like it's coming from *under* the floor. Jimmy, can you and Tex find something to use as a lever? The mortar is soft. We can use a rock or something to dig it out and then pry up the stone and see what's under there."

"Dirt," Tex barked with a laugh. "All that's under them stones is Carson Corners dirt."

"The sounds must be coming from somewhere," Alice said with a yawn.

"Let's find out where," Jimmy said with a smile. John used a rock and a trowel they found on the basement shelves to dig away at the mortar. Ten minutes later, using the coal shovel as a lever and putting all their combined weight into it, they lifted the stone from the floor. As the slab of rock tilted upward, John and Alice slid several loose bricks from the back of the store under the stone. After resting only a moment with the slab teetering on the bricks, everyone cupped their fingers under the stone and moved it out of the way.

"Tex is just pretending to lift," Walter groaned.

"Am not!"

"Get it over to the side," Jimmy grunted and they all eased the piece of stone out of the way. Dust and trails of loose rock slid into a hole under the cellar floor.

"It's hollow," John gasped. "Might lead to China."

"There's something down there," Walter said and Jimmy brought the oil lamp closer. "It's a trunk."

Jimmy reached out and started digging through the dirt, rubbing his fingers along the edges of the small chest. Tex chuckled. "Might want to watch them fingers, Jim. Could be a mess of snakes down there."

"Help me." Jimmy gripped the handle and started pulling. Walter, John and Alice all used their fingers to dig away until the chest came loose from the earth. They reached down and helped lift it up into the cellar. A wave of moist dirt came with it as it slid up onto the stone floor. Brushing their fingers over the top, they cleared away the soil. The trunk was a perfect cube, three feet in every direction. A stout old lock secured the metal box.

"Wow, it's like buried treasure." John giggled. Tex made a small sound in the back of his throat that showed he was very interested. Walter examined the metal box under the oil lamp. He pressed his nose almost to the surface while under the hurricane glass the flame wavered back and forth.

"It's not more than twenty years old. Maybe thirty."

"Could be something valuable, right?" Tex asked.

"I guess," he shrugged. "Depends on what's inside."

"Well, Tex?" Jimmy laughed. "Since you were so keen to pick a lock, that's the one to crack."

"Stand back, give me some room," Tex said. He sat down in front of the chest and gave it the once-over. Removing a small piece of metal from the lining of his overalls, he made a clucking sound and then went to work on the padlock.

"What was here before *Goode's*?" Jimmy asked. Alice and John shrugged.

"It's probably some land grants, deeds, confederate stuff from the Civil War," Walter said. "All worthless junk, I'd wager."

"No buried treasure?" John asked and Walter shook his head.

"I'm afraid not, Big John. We might get lucky and a few gold coins could be in there, but don't get your hopes up."

"I heard a story one time," John whispered, "about a man who chopped up his wife and buried the pieces around his farm. That box looks big enough for a head and some arms."

"You're making that up," Alice moaned, but she noticed how John slid around to her side, his hand tugging at her hip.

"Norbert Pearson told me about it."

"He's a liar."

"Sure would explain the noises," John said. "It's some poor spook wailing in the night 'cause their remains are crammed down in a metal box."

"Got it," Tex shouted. He looked over with a huge grin on his face and the padlock swinging from the metal hook. "Y'all wanna come on over and take a look?"

"We're fine from here," Jimmy gulped.

"Yep, we're good," Walter chimed in and realized he had taken a large step backward. Alice and John sidled back as well, their heads churning with thoughts of dried, decaying body parts inside the box. They were all glad Tex was the one sitting on the floor with the box between his legs. He looked confident to handle it.

"What if it really is...?" Jimmy whispered to Alice, but couldn't finish his thought. It was too gruesome.

"Tex will lose those ribs he had for supper. He'll maybe pass out or something. That's all."

"I can live with that," Jimmy shrugged. He yelled across the cellar. "Open her up, Tex!"

"You're all a bunch of chickens," Tex laughed. "It ain't gonna blow up."

Tex peeled back the rusty lid and held the oil lamp close. He glanced over at them with a sour face. "You're gonna love it, Walter."

"What is it?"

"Books," Tex snarled getting to his feet and brushing the dirt off his overalls. Walter strolled over with the rest of them. Inside the chest were dozens of leather-bound books with gold scrollwork across them. Walter sat down by the chest. The smell of freshly dug earth wafted from the hole in the ground. He picked up a book and brushed his hand over the dusty cover. A large leather strap had been attached to the spine and ran across the front of the book, secured with a heavy buckle.

"Wonder why they would do this?" he asked pulling the strap through the buckle and unfastening the belt. He opened the pages of the book once they were free of the strap and the leather binding creaked and groaned. The pages were fragile, as thin as snowflakes. Walter turned to the title page. In neat black lettering it read:

A History of the Revolutionary War.

John and Alice sat down beside the trunk and pulled out some of the books.

"Why are these belts attached?" Alice asked and Walter made an odd face. After a moment's silence, he glanced over and shrugged.

"I don't know. It doesn't make much sense unless they're all from some kind of collection. Look at all these wonderful old pictures: maps, drawings, letters from British soldiers."

"Boring," Tex groaned, flopping back down on the clothes

across the room with a huff. "Ain't nothing but a bunch of crummy old books."

"Afraid you might learn something, Tex?" Walter mumbled.

"Can I see that one?" Jimmy asked. Walter nodded, handing him the book on the Revolutionary War while digging back inside the chest.

"Will you read this to me, Alice?" John asked after getting the strap free from another book and holding it out. In gold lettering, the discolored title page read: *Peter Pan* by J.M. Barrie.

"Sure," Alice mumbled flipping through the thin pages. "Looks like it's the original play from 1904. This was long before it became a book, I think."

Jimmy put down *A History of the Revolutionary War* and pulled out another book. The strap was tight, but he managed to tug until it popped free. For a moment, the room seemed to be haunted with the smell of salt water and, for just a second, he thought he heard seagulls. Walter, Alice and John were too engrossed in the books to notice. He shook his head, thinking it must have been his imagination, but the scent was definitely there.

"You smell that?"

Walter looked up and turned his nose into the air. He sniffed for a moment and then looked back at Jimmy with a curious smile.

"Fish?"

"What book is that?" Alice asked.

Jimmy glanced down and then held it out to her. The first page was covered by an old ink sketch showing a whaling ship on the ocean. She took a moment to imagine the ship sailing somewhere fanciful like the West Indies, the hull sliding through the deep blue of the Sargasso Sea. Above it, spiky gold lettering spelled: *Moby Dick* by Herman Melville.

"Y'all gonna look at those creepy old books all night?" Tex grumbled from the other side of the cellar. "Douse that light and let a fella get some shut-eye, will ya?"

"When did anything like that ever bother you?" Jimmy giggled. "I've seen you hook your belt to the undercarriage, ride cross country in the rain and still snooze. You're never one for chasing sleep."

Walter brushed a fine layer of silt and dirt from another book and noticed a crucifix had been jammed against the pages of the book. The leather strap was old and stiff and had almost molded around the tarnished silver of the crucifix. He pushed and pulled until he undid the strap, peeled the crucifix from the book and threw open the pages. He had been sure Jimmy was exaggerating about the copy of *Moby Dick*. There was no way the smell of the ocean had actually entered the room. He knew more than likely the combination of upturned soil, old leather and the musty pages had created what *seemed* like the smell of salt and sea. As the crucifix fell into his lap though, he was almost certain he heard wolves howling in the distance. Looking up, he realized everyone else heard it too. Tex, already asleep, snored like a lumberjack, but the others looked around with odd expressions.

"Must be dogs," Jimmy shrugged, looking back down at the book cradled in his lap. John nodded.

"Something got them riled up."

Walter looked down at the faded pages and his eyes found the title of the book: *Dracula.*

He closed the leather cover and pocketed the crucifix. "Maybe we ought to go," Walter said. Jimmy looked up with a puzzled frown.

"Why?"

"Well, why do you think we all heard sounds coming from inside this trunk? I mean, it was buried down here for a reason, right?"

"They're just books," Jimmy chuckled, clapping a hand on Walter's shoulder.

"I know, but they're books with leather belts and buckles built right in. Why would someone do that?"

"Just like you said...some kind of collection."

"Yeah, but-"

Walter's voice dropped off as some sort of commotion began outside. Alice reached over and turned the flame on the lamp down until it vanished, leaving them in darkness. The sounds of their breathing echoed in the black while Tex snored. A moment passed and then two. The door to the cellar rattled. Through the cracks between the brick and the old wooden door, a soft pale light filtered through. It shimmered and flickered. Shuffling sounds continued in the alleyway for several minutes and then moved on, the pale, greenish light fading away. Jimmy breathed out a sigh and fumbled for a book of matches in his overalls. He struck one and the spark lit the oil lamp again. He replaced the glass globe and they all stared at each other. Jimmy got up, climbed the steps and unlocked the door.

"Maybe you shouldn't-" Walter started but Jimmy had already slipped out the door. Alice, John and Walter stood frozen in the lamplight's glow. Tex snored like a freight train.

Jimmy stood just outside the door in the alley. Snow drifted from the sky. Too dazed to move, he stood in a patch of freshly fallen snow for a moment until his brain jumped into action and he crept down the alley. At the corner of the building, he poked his head out and saw people milling around the square. A group of men talking all tipped their top hats as a woman walked by with a long velvet cloak. A woman in a thin wrap sold a handful of what looked like daisies to a young woman in a bustle skirt and mink bonnet. He stared at the strange scene for a moment and then ran back into the alley. A moment later, he entered the door with an odd look.

"Folks are moving along Main Street."

"It's the dead of night," John stammered.

Jimmy sighed. "I know, but I swear on a box of jam nuts, I can see people out there and get this...it's snowing."

"What?" Walter asked.

John's face went wild. "Hot dog! Can we go sledding?"

"Wait a minute," Walter said, "It can't be snowing. It wasn't *that* cold when we came into town. It never snows this early around here."

"I'm telling you, it's really coming down. There's got to be three inches on the ground already and it's plenty cold. Feels like its dropped twenty degrees in just a few hours."

"You don't have to go, do you?" Alice asked with a frown.

"Nah, I'll stay," Jimmy smiled. "There's some weird stuff going on though. Those people look like...I don't know, like they're all dressed up. Like pictures I've seen in books."

"And what was that light? It wasn't like anything I've ever seen," Alice whispered.

Jimmy looked over at Walter and shrugged. "Okay, why don't you and Tex get back to the train yard and stay put. I'll be back by morning."

"If people are out there," Walter began, "then somebody might try to get in here.

"We'll bolt the door from the inside," Jimmy said. "Besides, if all these strange things are happening here, I'd rather you and Tex check out the jungle. Make sure Old Willie and the folks there are all right."

"But what if their aunt decides to check on them? If she finds you here-"

"I'll hide in the back under some boxes or clothes or stuff. Let's wake Tex and you guys get going."

After they explained what was happening, Tex looked at them for a long moment and then broke into a wail of laughter. Walter clamped a hand over his mouth and stared at the door, but there was no movement. "I told you he wouldn't believe us."

Tex slapped Walter's hand away with a chuckle. "So, let me get this here story straight...you all saw a light moving around the door and heard the handle rattle and it's snowing and we're going back to the train yard?"

"Yep," Jimmy nodded. "That's about the size of it."

"Y'all are a bunch of scaredy-cats. Every town in this country has a night watchman or a sheriff and he walks around checking to make sure everything is locked up. It was probably a light from a lantern. And unless the world's done gone crazy, snow ain't nothing to be afraid of."

"There are people out all over town in the middle of the night," Walter said with a stern face. Tex looked at him for a moment, opened his mouth, closed it and then shrugged.

"Maybe it's a party?"

"Well, I guess," Walter mumbled. Jimmy looked at him like he was as crazy as a bedbug. Walter adjusted his glasses and cleared his throat. "I'm just saying it's possible. You said they were all dressed up. Maybe it's the town's centennial or something."

"Help me get this hole covered up," Jimmy said, kneeling on the floor and starting to dump the books back into the chest.

"Don't bury it again," John whined. "Alice is gonna read me some of those."

Jimmy and Walter dropped the books in the chest and slid it over to the side. Alice draped a piece of old cloth over the top while Tex, Walter and Jimmy slid the stone back into place, covering the hole in the floor.

"Okay, get going," Jimmy pressed, shoving Tex and Walter toward the door. "Here, take some candles. Don't stop to chat with anyone. Get back to the train yard and I'll be there by dawn. I want to stay and make sure Alice and John are safe. If anything happens, we'll meet back here tomorrow evening after dark. Got it?"

"Check," Walter sighed. "Alice, I hope you don't mind, but I was hoping I could borrow a few books?"

"Of course I don't mind. Take whatever you want."

"Thanks," Walter grinned, tapping the pages of one of the books he pulled from his coat. "I always meant to read

Great Expectations. Dickens is such a fine writer. I borrowed *Oliver Twist* and *Dracula* as well."

Jimmy threw open the door, glanced outside at the snow drifting from the black clouds above them and signaled to Walter and Tex. Walter slammed the copy of *Great Expectations* closed and stuffed it back inside his coat along with several other books. Tex waved good-bye, yawning. A blast of cold air hit his face and he shivered. Jimmy bolted the door behind them.

Walking through the snow, Tex and Walter reached the alleyway and peered out. The square was empty. Snow had covered the street and the sidewalks.

"Ain't nobody out here," Tex grumbled. "Let's go back inside where it's warm."

"Look," Walter said pointing to the ground. Dozens of footprints in the snow lined the sidewalks. "There were people here. Lots of them. If the snow keeps up for another hour or so, there won't be any prints left."

"Well, if there were people around...where'd they go?"

Walter shrugged and then shivered in the cold. They walked down the street, keeping close to the buildings and the shadows that fell from the awnings.

———

"What did they look like? The people you saw outside?" Alice whispered after John had drifted off to sleep. Her brother was curled on his side, clutching one of the books they had found from the trunk in his arms, the pages curling against his chest. The cover had large gold letters reflecting in the dim light. It read: *Dinosaurs, A History of Prehistoric*

Times. Jimmy looked over in the dark and could barely make out her face.

"They were dressed like people from one of the matinees we use to see down at the Victory. Back in Boise, Tex and Walter and I would sneak into the back of the old theater and catch a picture show. They looked like people from England a hundred years ago."

"A hundred years ago?" Alice repeated, but he made no response and she couldn't see him in the darkness. "Strange," Jimmy muttered sometime later. Alice could tell she was falling asleep because his voice sounded distant. In her dreams, horse-drawn carriages rumbled through her sleep and people in top hats and tails and silky long skirts walked the streets of foggy London town.

Chapter Five

A Night Visitor

Walter sat huddled against the boxcar wall in the field behind the train yard. Tex grumbled again about how cold he was while slipping an extra coat over his chest to act as a blanket. He curled up in the corner and belched.

"I don't see why we had to leave," he complained. Walter lit a candle. He set it down beside him and the interior of the train car came to life with faint, flickering shadows. Outside snow still fell from the darkness. "You ain't gonna read at a time like this, are ya'?"

"Why not?"

"'Cause I need my beauty rest."

"Too late."

"I ought to bust you over the head," Tex growled. "Jimmy too. He played us something good. Making up stories about people out in the snow and then getting us to leave so he could stay all bundled up with his new sweetheart. 'Oh Alice, you're soooo pretty!' 'Oh Jimmy, you're dreamy!' Makes me wanna loose my supper."

"There were folks outside the store or there wouldn't have been footprints."

"You're a smart kid, Walter. How could all the prints be there and the people just up and vanished?"

"What are you saying?"

"Jimmy went out and stomped around in the snow and made those prints himself. He wanted some quiet time with his new skirt."

"Have you ever known Jimmy to tell a lie? C'mon, Tex, don't be a thickhead. Here, I brought you a book," Walter said, with some irritation. He pulled out one of the leather books and slid it across the floor. Tex glanced at the title for a moment and then smiled.

"Thanks, Walt. You're all right."

"I know how you like gunslingers and the old west. I thought you might practice reading while you're at it, not just looking at the pictures."

"'Night," Tex muttered, tucking the book under his bindle for extra head support. He turned over with his back to the cold doorway. Walter slipped one of the leather books to the floor and flipped it open. He was a little hesitant after what had happened back in the cellar, but then tried to tell himself it was all a strange coincidence. There were no wolves in North Carolina. It had been old country dogs howling out in the distance.

The bells in the court square tower chimed three. Walter glanced up and wasn't sure if he had fallen asleep or not, but the pages were a little sticky and so was his face. He thought he must have been drooling. The cold wind whistled by the car door. Walter stared out into the wintry landscape. Pine trees with branches laden heavy with snow held dark and silent secrets inside the forests. The candle had been blown out by the wind and the train car was dark, but the night was brightened by the glow coming off the powdery snow.

Walter shuffled, sitting up against the cold metal sides of the car. He heard Tex snoring and could just barely make out the shape of his body covered in a pale bluish splash of light. A sound from somewhere inside the boxcar made him go numb with fear. It was only a shuffling sound, but he realized someone else was there with them.

"Jimmy?" he whispered.

Silence.

"Somebody here?"

"Forgive my intrusion," a voice floated from the darkness. It was a deep voice with a strange accent he couldn't place.

"Hi there," Walter said squinting his eyes to try and see anything, any kind of movement, but it was no use. Only darkness stared back at him from the corners. "You just get in on a night freighter?"

"Where am I?"

"You're in North Carolina, mister. Carson Corners."

"The colonies?"

"Yes," Walter said after a brief pause. *They're not colonies anymore*, he thought. *They're states now. What a funny thing to ask.* He started to feel chills run up and down his spine—and not from the cold. Something strange had happened. He couldn't explain it, but he could feel it. The inside of the boxcar smelled funny, like something dead. "Where you headed?"

"This will do," the voice whispered.

"There'll be coffee and maybe some stale rolls for breakfast in a few hours."

"I do feel...very hungry."

Walter didn't like the way those words came rolling out with such a sense of *need*. He reached into his overalls and pulled out a box of matches he always kept tucked inside. He fumbled with the first match and couldn't get a spark, but got the second one lit. He felt around for the stub of the candle. He lit the match to the wick. The interior of the boxcar brightened, but only a little. A dark figure stepped forward from the corner of the boxcar and Walter went cold inside. He couldn't feel his body. He couldn't move. The long, tattered folds of the black, wool cloak dragged along the dirty ground as a wall of heavy black Victorian clothing overwhelmed him. The figure knelt down in front of the candle's flame.

Walter turned his gaze upward and studied the face in the pale candlelight. Tiny bits of stubble darkened the jaw line. It looked like tiny black ants inside a bowl of chalky-white flour. The man, if you could call him that, wasn't ugly at all. He was oddly handsome with shaggy dark hair that made him seem more wolfish. The eyes were the worst—black with tiny flecks of red that caught the candle's flame. The creature smiled and Walter wanted to scream. He wanted to open his mouth and scream louder and longer than he ever had, but couldn't. All his muscles locked. The man's teeth were the color of ancient ivory. The fangs dipped below the other teeth and the points touched his bottom lip. A tongue appeared, black with decay. And Walter knew it

71

wasn't decay like you'd see from time to time traveling the rails, when a skunk or possum killed on the side of the tracks was stinking to high heaven for all it was worth. This was *eternal* rot.

"What's your name?" the creature asked. Walter smelled the horrid breath. He found his voice and pulled it from the back of his throat. It came out tiny and breathless, his words stuttering.

"W-Walter G-Grisbee, sir."

He dropped his eyes from the monster's pallid face and oily hair. Walter glanced at the book he had left open on the floor of the train car. He knew all too well who was sitting on his haunches not more than three feet away. *The book*, Walter thought. *Somehow when I opened the book, he came out into the world. What have I done?* He swallowed the taste of fear, as acrid as castor oil, and glanced up to face Count Dracula.

"Tell me, Walter, do you know how I came to be here?"

He couldn't find the words.

"I think you do," the Count purred in his rich accent. His dark eyes flickered over to Tex and then slid back. "Perhaps I should wake him?"

"Nah, he's just a kid," Walter shrugged trying to sound casual. He slid to one side, trying to cover the book with the tail of his coat, but the Count saw him. Reaching down with one claw-like hand, he snagged the leather binding. Walter stared at the hands. They were thin and long and dirt lay embedded under the long, curved nails. The pale skin showed a strange bluish tint under the bloodless flesh. A silver ring tarnished black from age sat on the index finger of the right hand. His dark eyes twitched.

"I think you know who I am indeed," the Count growled, gazing at the title scribbled in gold at the top of the leather book. "There will be an accident under one of the morning trains. Did you know that? There won't be any blood, but that's a small thing, tiny by nature. No one will be looking for blood. They'll find only pieces anyway."

Walter patted his coat pocket until his fingers curled around the crucifix he had pulled from the book. He brought it out of his coat pocket, fumbling as he did so, and the crucifix immediately cast a strange light inside the train car. The Count retreated, clutching the book to his chest. His eyes turned wild. A feral snarl broke from his lips and he threw himself out of the train car into the snow, his cape billowing in the wind. Walter waited a long moment and then peered outside. There was no one there. The snow set in heaps, undisturbed. Tex still snored away, unaware of what had happened. Walter sat up all night, the crucifix in his hand. When pale daylight brightened the sky, he woke Tex and began telling him everything that had happened.

"You are one crazy kangaroo," Tex laughed. Sometime just before dawn, the snow had stopped, but the icy cold day was still overcast and thick clouds puffed along the skyline.

"You don't believe me?"

"Believe that some blood sucker came out of a book?"

"You think I imagined it?"

"You were dreaming."

"It wasn't a dream! He was here last night! I saw him. I smelled him. Remember that fruit harvest that went bad in

Salinas? The one we worked last autumn?"

Tex rolled his eyes. "Why don't we see if we can get somethin' to eat?"

"He smelled like that...sweet, but rotting. Like old apples."

"You can tell Jimmy all about it when he gets back. Well, that's *if* he gets back. He might be married by now," Tex scowled.

"You think I'm making it up?"

"No, but a nightmare can *seem* mighty real. After all, I was there and didn't hear a thing."

"You'd sleep through an earthquake," Walter snorted climbing down from the boxcar. His feet landed in the powdery snow with a plop. "Besides, its morning and Jimmy's not back. I'm going to the department store to have a look. You want to come along?"

Tex shrugged with a huff. "Fine, but do me a favor? Stop talking about ghosties and ghoulies, okay?"

When Walter and Tex reached town, they loitered on the corner of Main and Willowby, watching people moving in and out of the storefronts. Sidewalks were being swept clean of the snow. They looked at each other and strolled down the sidewalk, hopping over the mound of snow brushed into the gutter until they could see the corner of *Goode's Mercantile*. Three figures were off to the side of the alley.

"There they are," Tex said. Walter and Tex ran to the corner, all smiles.

"Hey, fellas!" Jimmy waved as they came racing up.

Jimmy was eating an apple and standing with his back to the wall while Alice and John stood at his side.

"Where have you been?" Walter demanded.

"I stayed to help Alice and John get the boiler going this morning."

"It's burning up down there," Alice sighed, wiping a line of sweat from her forehead. "We needed some fresh air."

"What are you guys doing here?" Jimmy asked.

"Starvin'?" Tex mumbled. Jimmy handed over the rest of his apple and Tex buried his teeth into the green apple with a hearty crunch. Walter frowned.

"Jimmy, when we left last night, Main Street was empty. There wasn't a soul in sight."

"That's impossible. There were a dozen folks wandering around."

"They were all gone. We found footprints in the snow, but that was it. We didn't see anyone all the way back to the train yard, but late last night something happened. You know those books I borrowed from Alice and John? The ones we found under the floor?"

"What happened?" Alice asked.

"I started reading—"

"Oh, here we go again," Tex snarled, tossing the apple core into the snow of the alley.

Walter whirled on him. "You said I could tell Jimmy all about it! Well, that's exactly what I'm going to do, Tex. So you just stand there and keep your trap shut."

"Easy, fellas," Jimmy hushed, pulling them away from the building and farther into the street. He glanced around behind him to see if anyone had heard. Mr. Yules, the second halt of *Morton & Yules, Undertakers*, stared through his big glass windows hung with heavy velvet drapes. He turned away with a stony face. Alice and John gathered closer around and the five of them huddled on the edge of the street. Walter began relating his story. People moved around them, a horse and buggy got a wheel stuck in the snow not more than fifty feet away and the bell in the court square tower chimed, but none of them heard anything except Walter's fantastic tale. When he finished, Jimmy had one corner of his lip tucked under his teeth, Alice was looking upward into the sky with a serious frown and John was staring at him with wide eyes. Tex chuckled and broke the silence.

"Walter had a big, scary dream is all."

"He took the book with him," Walter continued, ignoring Tex. His eyes stared at Jimmy, pleading. "He's gone, vanished into the darkness. He could be anywhere."

"Who's Dracula?" John asked.

"A vampire," Walter said. "He's hundreds of years old."

"A few years back, we snuck in to see the picture show," Jimmy said with a grimace. "That was spring of '31. He had a thick accent and turned into a bat. He drank people's blood to survive. They drove a stake through his heart in the end."

"I remember that," Tex laughed. "That fella in the penguin suit and cape? Did he have a cape, Walt? Was it just like the picture show?"

"Yes, he had a cape, but it was thick and moldy. He had sharp teeth, like a wolf. His eyes were all dark and kinda like liquid. It was scarier than the movie. Much scarier! He was so...real."

Alice swallowed and her breath came out in pale, wispy trails in the morning cold. "What are we going to do?"

"Something happened," Jimmy said. "We opened those books and something happened. I don't know what, but it's the only thing that makes sense. Remember the smells? And I know, without a doubt, I saw those people last night."

"You're gonna go along with this?" Tex asked, facing Jimmy. Walter pulled his hands from his pockets and grabbed Tex by the arms. He spun him around and faced him.

"Tex, it wasn't a dream. Jimmy saw people out here wandering around in the night. It started snowing out of nowhere. The Count was in the train car. I saw him, spoke to him, smelled him. And I'll tell you something else—he was *hungry*."

"Are all those books closed?" Jimmy asked. Alice's eyes grew wide with alarm.

"Not all of them. John was looking through them this morning."

"We have to get them closed and back in that trunk. Alice?"

Jimmy followed her gaze, but saw only the front of the store with people moving in and out of the doors. Icicles hung from the rooftops and the gray, overcast sky looked like a painted backdrop.

"Alice, what is it?"

"Miss Goode." All of them faced the store and found her thin, short frame at the windows of the second floor. She stared down at them with her one beady black eye.

"Look over this way," Alice said and directed her gaze

down the street. She extended her arm and everyone turned their attention down the snow-covered lane at the buildings. They stood for a moment and then Tex whispered to Walter.

"What are we looking at?"

"I'm giving you directions," Alice hissed. "Just in case anyone asks, you stopped for directions."

"Why don't we meet back up tonight and see if we can't figure out what's going on," Jimmy announced. "Alice, you know anyone that can help us?"

"I'll think on it. Go! Hurry before she gets suspicious."

Walter, Tex and Jimmy all tipped their caps and walked off in the direction Alice had pointed, leaving her and John in the street. A moment later, Alice wrapped her arm around her brother's shoulder and guided him back toward the store without daring to look up at the windows. She was not certain if Miss Goode was still there, but she felt that cold eye on them until they slipped into the shadow of the alley. They both hurried into the coal cellar and the stifling heat from the boiler, shutting the door behind them.

An hour later, Alice was shoveling coal into the boiler and John was cleaning off some of the shelves when they heard the key rattling in the lock. The door opened and Miss Goode stood with the key ring in her hand. Rufus sat beside her on his haunches.

"Good afternoon," she said, offering them a thin smile. John said nothing; he went back to work. Alice slipped from the boiler room.

"Miss Goode," she acknowledged with a stiff nod.

"I thought I would come down and check on you. It's

the least I could do."

"We're fine," Alice said.

"I see," she nodded. "You've made a vast improvement in this cellar in only a few days. Looks clean enough to live in. You're getting your meals at night?"

"Yes, ma'am."

"Where did these oil lamps come from?"

"We found them," Alice lied. "We cleaned out some of the boxes in the back and found those."

"And the oil?"

"Ma'am?"

"The oil that goes in them," Miss Goode snapped. She turned on the heels of her black shoes and stared at Alice. "Where did you get the *oil*?"

"We traded for it," John said, patting down his shirt and overalls. A thin layer of dust and soot came wafting off his clothing and floated in the air. "We went down to the train yard and found some hobos willing to do some dickering. All they wanted in return was some old milk bottles we found."

Miss Goode said nothing, but clicked her tongue against the roof of her mouth. She pursed her bright red lips and walked into the back of the cellar. Alice held her breath when the black, thick heels hit the piece of stone they had moved. Miss Goode paused almost as if trying to determine if the slab of stone were loose. Alice glanced into the far corner of the room where an old piece of cloth covered the small metal trunk.

"Is there anything else, Miss Goode?" Alice asked with her heart racing. The woman turned and brought a hand to her head, smoothing invisible stray hairs from her forehead.

"It's warm down here."

"Yeah, it gets hot," John laughed.

"Since you've been to the train yards, you know we have a lot of shiftless, lazy bums around town. They come looking for handouts. It's shameful. They even approached my home once. Only once, mind you. I called the police on them."

"How brave," John mumbled.

"What did you say?"

Alice jumped in. "We met some of those hobos this morning, as a matter of fact. Some of them were asking for work. We told them they could keep walking. We said there might be some kind of work farther down Main, but not around *Goode's Mercantile*. No, sirree. We told them the owner doesn't cater to charity cases."

Miss Goode looked Alice over with a steady eye and then nodded. "Excellent. That's exactly what you should tell them, all of them."

The heat began to affect Miss Goode. She pulled a linen hanky from her pocket and dabbed at her neck and across her forehead above the eye patch. Marching across the room, she mounted the steps and stood in the doorway of the stairwell.

"That's a little better. It's so stuffy. Listen here, both of you, has anything odd happened while you've been living down here?"

John and Alice looked at each other in silence.

"What I mean is—the cellar is old and it's bound to play tricks on your eyes and ears, but there's nothing to be afraid of down here. Is that clear?"

"Yes ma'am," they said in unison.

"If anything happens, I want you to tell me immediately. Do you understand?"

"Of course," Alice said.

"It's just so strange...the snow this early in the fall. And Rufus started barking last night. He fixed himself in one spot and wouldn't move. He glared due north for an hour and barked nonstop. I couldn't even get him to quiet down for some steak bones."

John and Alice looked at each other again. Miss Goode licked her lips and gave them a final nod. She closed the door and they heard the rusty key in the lock, followed by her footsteps and Rufus's paws on the stairs. Alice turned to her brother and her face was grim. "She knows."

Chapter Six

America Earns its Freedom...Again

Bob Craven sat on the bottom of the stairs leading toward the alley. The wind howled outside and the lamplight cast strange shadows over the cellar. The boiler was dying out, but the last trail of fire still flickered in the grate. Walter, Tex, John, Jimmy and Alice sat on the floor staring up at him. They had just finished telling him everything that had happened. At first, he was shocked to learn Walter, Tex and Jimmy had stayed down in the cellar, but after hearing everything else that happened, his expression had turned to stone.

Tex smiled. "As you can tell, mister, my friends are a wee bit short of a sackful up top."

"Where are they?" Bob asked.

"Where's what?" Tex stammered.

"The books!"

"Over here," Alice said. Bob jumped from his spot and

slid into the corner of the cellar. Ripping back the cloth, he threw open the metal box and began sorting through them with nimble fingers.

"What are you looking for?" John asked kneeling beside Bob.

"I was just...I wanted to see if ....never mind."

Alice put a hand on Bob's shoulder. "You are the only adult we know around here. We were hoping you would help us."

Bob looked up and smiled. He dropped to the cold floor in a way she found rather odd. He seemed defeated and his eyes were haunted, but he nodded. "Of course I'll help you. It would be a sad day indeed for someone to hear a story like that and not help such courageous children."

Tex shook his head in disbelief. "You believe that load of malarkey?"

"It's all true."

"It can't be!" Tex stammered. "Now I might be twelve, but I know monsters ain't real."

"Depends on how you look at it really. You're right that monsters aren't real...but they can be *made* to be real. These are not all the books. There are more of them...hidden somewhere. And, yes, Alice you and John were correct with your assumptions: Miss Goode knows."

"You're as wacky as they are!" Tex said and plopped on the floor, throwing his cap down beside him. Bob Craven offered a thin smile.

"I'm afraid it's happened before."

"When? You saw it?" Jimmy asked.

"I've worked for Miss Goode almost thirty years now.

She's an awful woman, no doubt about it. Anyone around here will tell you as much. Many years ago she came into possession of these books. I don't know how they work, what kind of magic makes them the way they are and, frankly, I don't want to know. It's enough to understand the books are alive. I know that makes me sound rather daffy, Tex, but it's true. They're like ghosts. The voices and sounds you heard are the books: snippets of dialogue, little bits of description leaking out. Fragments of the books have been haunting this cellar, wanting to get out because when you open the books, the characters see a window into this world. Like a tiny spark of light. All they have to do is follow and they're not ghosts any more, not just words on a page. They are as real as you and I."

"What have we done?" Alice groaned.

"It's not *your* fault," Bob stressed. "That awful woman must have assumed she could bury these books under the floor and that would be the end of it. The ones you found she must have deemed too dangerous to keep in her possession. Or maybe there just wasn't a way to exploit them. Whatever the reason, she must have sealed them up and buried them years ago never thinking anyone would know the difference."

"So, there are other books like these?" Walter asked.

"Yes, many of them. The books don't just allow characters to come out. You can use the books, actually withdraw things from the novels. As long as you can get a character to go back and forth into the pages for you, then anything that's been described in the novel can be made real. That's how she's as rich as she is now. She convinced characters to go into the books and bring her things. She's been stealing from the pages for years: jewels, gold, valuables."

"The people I saw," Jimmy started, "the ones last night in the snow? I saw them clear as day and then five minutes later Tex and Walter saw no one. What happened?"

"Ah, well…I don't know for certain," Bob said, scratching the tiny white trail of stubble on his chin. "Most of the time, the main characters are the ones that emerge. The author has spent more time developing those characters and so they're stronger. They usually emerge faster than some of the others, but not always. Every book is different. Sometimes, the eager characters or ones with just plain, brute strength come bursting through. It could be the people you saw were just background characters, little more than a brief description of a scene, just a line or two. They might have been there for a moment and then when you closed a book, they were gone."

"Makes sense," Walter nodded. "They were not full-fledged characters so they couldn't exist for long."

"That's right," Bob agreed. "They could have never survived here because no one wrote enough of a life for them. They were only shadow-people."

"So," Jimmy said, "what I saw was like looking at a photograph."

"Yes, exactly. A moving one, though. Closing the books must have ended their lives."

"But Dracula was different," Walter mumbled.

Bob nodded gravely. Alice glanced around at their faces and then breathed a sigh. "Have you read *Dracula*?"

"Yes, many years ago," Bob said with a sad smile. "It was

a bit lurid, but I always had an affinity for British authors."

"Me too," Walter said.

"Really?"

"I was going to read *Great Expectations*, but now I won't be able to open it again."

"I have a copy I can let you borrow," Bob announced with a bubbling smile. "It's not Dickens's best work by far, but I think you'll enjoy it."

"Well, ain't that nice?" Tex said. "You two have something in common. Maybe y'all should sit around and form a book club like women of high society? You can have cakes and tea and parties. You can talk about books all day!"

"Back to business, I suppose." Bob sighed. "We need to make a list of all the books you've opened and roughly how long they were open. Now don't look so glum. We might just have a way out of this."

"How do you mean?" Alice asked.

"If we can get close enough, we can get the characters back into the books."

"Is that true?"

"Oh yes. They have to make contact with the books."

"But the Count touched the book and nothing happened," Walter said.

"Well...did he touch the pages?"

"No, just the cover. He picked it up by the spine."

"That explains it then. The pages are where the power lies."

"How do you know all this?" Alice asked. All eyes shifted to where Bob sat in the lantern's glow. He cleared his throat and shrugged with a weak smile. He opened his mouth, but something hit the wooden door to the alley with a loud crack. Alice screamed and all of them bounced to their feet. They stood silent for a few moments and then the sound echoed again, louder and stronger than before.

"What was that?" John hissed, inching closer to Jimmy and Walter. They all began backing up toward the boiler room.

"Mr. Craven," Jimmy whispered. "Books might have been open for periods of time and nothing would happen, right?"

"It's p-possible," he stuttered.

"Well, I opened *Moby Dick* and the whale didn't come swimming out."

"Maybe it takes longer for some of them to find their way out," Walter mumbled.

"He's probably right," Bob said, still keeping his voice low. "Some of them have to manifest a way."

"What's that mean?" Tex asked.

"They have to make their own way into this world. Adapt."

"Sorry, I don't have one clue what you said, mister," Tex snapped.

The door to the cellar was hit hard. All of them jumped.

"Something's trying to get in," Alice whispered. "Bob, can you get us upstairs into the store?"

Bob began fumbling for his keys. He leaped up the steps and began twirling the keys on his ring, trying to find the right one. All of them crowded in behind him, turning to watch the door to the alley in case it gave way.

"What about the books?" Jimmy asked.

"Bring them with us," Bob yelled. Jimmy and Tex jumped

down and ran over, hoisting the chest with them back to the front of the cellar.

"Here it is," Bob announced and then groaned. "No, that's the wrong one."

"Can you hurry up?" Tex asked.

The door was hit again and they all heard a crack in the wood.

"It's not gonna hold."

"This one doesn't fit the lock," Bob mumbled.

"Alice, I'm scared!" John yelled, pressing against his sister.

"It's okay, John. Everything will be fine."

"I'm sorry. I don't ever come down this way. I'm not sure I've ever used this lock. Maybe it's this old key here."

"The wood's cracking!" Jimmy spread his arms out across the others, thinking whatever was coming through would get him first and the others might be able to escape.

"Got it!" Bob shouted. As the key turned in the lock, the children fell through the doorway behind him, stumbling and rolling in the darkness of the stairwell. Jimmy dragged the chest in as the hinges screamed on the alley door. There was a sharp, ripping sound and the wood finally gave way. Jimmy slammed the door to the stairs shut and they all lay panting in the darkness. Shouts and heavy footsteps could be heard in the coal cellar and then pounding against the door. Alice, John and Walter all shouted in the darkness, fumbling to stand up. Jimmy felt someone's hand on his arm. He turned to move and fell over, hitting his head against a blunt object.

"I found the railing," Alice said. "We can get to the second level from here."

"No," Bob said. "Let's get in the side door."

A moment later, there was the jingling of keys and Bob opened the door to the ground floor of the store. Alice and John helped Jimmy, Walter and Tex stand up.

"Ouch," Jimmy groaned, rubbing his head. "I think I hit something."

"It was my head," Tex shouted. Bob helped pull the chest into the store and locked the door to the stairwell.

"There. They'll have to get through two more doors to reach us. We should be safe."

"It's so dark," Walter mumbled.

"I know," Bob agreed. "But we can't risk turning on the lights. Move over to your right and let's make our way to the front. There should be light near the windows."

"Who do you think broke in?" Walter asked, leaning closer to Bob Craven.

"I don't know. How long were those books open?"

"Some just a few seconds, but others were open...a good while," Alice answered, walking close behind them. Bob led them through the aisles to the front of the store. As they rounded the corner, they had a fantastic view of Main Street through the glass windows. At first, it looked like a fireworks celebration and then, as all of them inched closer, they realized what was happening. Walter and Alice pressed their hands against the glass with John, Tex and Jimmy following. Bob Craven walked up behind them and dropped a hand on Alice's shoulder. He was able to get only two words through his lips as they watched the events unfolding on Main Street.

"Oh dear," he muttered in shock.

That night in Carson Corners, the Revolutionary War began. Musket fire echoed through the streets and, throughout the town, people stepped to their front porches where they heard Minutemen calling them to arms. British Redcoats advanced through the streets. A poultry truck coming from Angus McMillan's farm was seized by the British. When they didn't understand how to operate the 'war ship', they accidentally drove the thing into a snowy ditch and five hundred chickens escaped into town.

Mrs. Edith Sinclair, age 74 and in poor health for the last decade, awoke from a calm sleep to find a British flag being nailed to her home. When she went outside in her nightgown to protest, two hundred yards away in the middle of the town square, the militia fired a field cannon. A small blast of smoke curled the air and a six-pound iron ball whizzed through the air, crashing into Mrs. Sinclair's parlor window. Screaming, she fled next door to the neighbor's where all of them hid in the root cellar until morning.

Ida and George Granger, both retired and living on the south side of town, sat on their front porch and cheered when the first gunfire erupted. They had a front row seat when Major John Pitcairn, leader of the British troops, yelled into the night, "Disperse, you damned rebels! You dogs, run!"

"Go get 'em, boys," Mrs. Granger yelled from the porch. A musket fired in the dark and the Minutemen jumped into action. The British troops advanced with bayonets and the Grangers cheered from their rockers. They stomped their feet. Mrs. Granger brought out some iced tea and homemade cherry pie.

Three miles away, Thomas Harman and Clyde Witherspoon, both veterans of the Civil War, waved the American flag and marched down the sidewalk.

Inside *Goode's Mercantile*, pale faces stared through the glass window at the spectacle along Main Street. The volunteer fire brigade pulled up, trying to block some of the British troops, who had already set fire to Cooper's Feed and Hardware Store. The firemen tried to douse the growing flames that lit up the night. Pistol shots were fired. Jimmy, Walter, Tex, John, Alice and Bob Craven all turned their heads in unison as a cannonball sailed down the street and smashed into Mr. Cannery's Model T Ford. The iron ball went right through the windshield and glass shattered all over the snow.

"Well," Jimmy mumbled. "That's something you don't see everyday."

"Yep," Alice calmly responded.

Minutemen, British Redcoats, and citizens of Carson Corners scrambled through the streets with chickens squawking and flapping in the dark and a relentless *pop-pop-pop* of pistols down the block. A cannonball shot through the marquee of the Diamond Palace and the lettering for *Barbary Coast* went flying into the dark. You could still read "Starring Edward G. Robinson" just below the shattered fragments of the marquee, but the light bulbs began to pop and fizzle and then everything went dark around the theater.

"You believe us now, right?" Walter asked, glancing over at Tex. The boy's mouth hung open and his eyes were wide and bright. He nodded without speaking. Walter looked at

Bob. "Can we stop all this?"

"I think so," he said, tearing his gaze from the war outside and then giving an enthusiastic nod. "I take that back—I'm *sure* we'll be able to stop it. We've just got to get close enough without getting shot. Where's the book on the Revolutionary War?"

All of them bent down and began shifting through the chest except John, who stood dumbfounded. He continued to stare out the window. A rumble echoed down the street and under the bronze street lamps another cannonball bounced through the snow, burying itself in the side of Walker's Drug Store.

"Here we go," Bob announced. He lifted the book and held it to his chest. "All right, I'm going out there and see if I can end this—"

The words died on his lips.

All of them turned and stared from the department store window. Silently and without warning, something black and monstrous moved from the alley between the police station and Grover's Fine Boutique directly across the street. They all saw it in shadow at first and then it lunged from the alley into the firelight. John screamed and jumped back. Everyone else followed, moving back from the glass, in awe of the size and sight of the Tyrannosaurus Rex. It was a good fifteen feet tall, not an adult yet, but the fierce black eyes gleamed in the light of the hardware store fire. His massive, block-shaped head floated left and right, then he drew back and his jaws opened. Teeth the size of railroad spikes gleamed in the shadows. He snapped his head down into the street, and latched his jaws onto a British Redcoat sneaking down the sidewalk. The man screamed for a moment and then he was gone, dragged backward. The dinosaur bounded back into the alley. Even though they didn't see it, they all knew by the giant shadows displayed on the alley walls what was happening.

"M-maybe we can find another w-w-way," Bob stammered.

"Yeah," Tex nodded, "where we don't have to get eaten."

"I can't believe it," Walter said in a dazed voice. "That was a Tyrannosaurus Rex! I've read about them. They've been extinct for millions of years."

"Not tonight," Jimmy added. "Now there's one across the street."

"You think there's more?" Walter asked curiously.

Bob groaned. "Oh, I hope not."

A cannonball exploded through the window twenty feet from Walter's head. All of them ducked and then looked to see the damage. Shards of glass hung from the frame, while tiny pieces caught the firelight across the floor. Outside, the Minutemen were running through the street, some engaging in hand-to-hand combat.

"That was close," Alice sighed.

"Gonna get closer," Jimmy yelled as a group of British officers stormed the door. Two heavy thrusts and the doors to *Goode's Mercantile* flew backward with the locks broken. British officers carried wounded men and weapons in out of the darkness. An officer with dark hair, slick with sweat, and buttons gleaming on his red uniform stepped up. His crisp, British accent poured out.

"Under the Quartering Act, you're required to relinquish

this building for British troops. Do you understand, sir?"

"Yes, of course," Bob answered. "We're loyal to the crown."

"Excellent! We require medical attention and food," he announced. Soldiers dropped bayonets, pistols and sabers in the doorway as they dragged wounded men in through the broken remains of the door. Soft moans and cries came from some of the bleeding men with makeshift bandages around their head, feet, arms and legs. Wounded men were lifted up on the piles of clothing stacked on tables.

"This is our chance," Jimmy whispered, nudging Bob with his arm. "These folks just fell in our laps."

Bob nodded and then spoke up. "I'm sorry, sir, my children and I were hiding out here. How goes the war?"

"We'll take them yet." He nodded, stalking off into the back of the store.

"Stay with me," Bob hissed and Tex, Jimmy, Alice, Walter and John all inched closer to Bob. "We'll try to get close enough to get them back into the book and not get pulled in ourselves."

"That can happen?" Alice asked with fear in her eyes.

"Oh, yes," Bob answered.

"We got ourselves a bigger problem," John said. Walter peered around the group to the front of the store.

"What is it? The Tyrannosaurus?"

"Almost as bad," John gulped.

The beige 1931 Packard Sedan came roaring up Main Street like a locomotive. The tires squealed to a halt in front of the store. Bob gasped and slid his arms protectively around the children. Effigy Goode kicked open the car door and crawled from the soft, tan leather interior with rage turning her face a bright pink. Her hair was loose, falling in black waves around the shoulders of her flowing, pink nightgown. She pulled a Winchester rifle from the backseat with a snarl.

"Oh, Good Lord," Bob managed just under his breath.

Miss Goode's Great Dane, Rufus, leaped from the passenger seat, his ears pointed straight up and his eyes alert. He turned his massive gray muzzle and sniffed the air still acrid with gunpowder. Miss Goode slopped through the snow in wet, pink bedroom slippers coated with dirty snow. She barreled up the sidewalk, teeth gritted tight and a long strand of hair curling into her face. Her eyes were wild. She stopped just outside the broken glass of the window and peered in with her lips curling back. When she saw them, she let out a growl that sounded inhuman.

"*WHAT HAVE YOU DONNNNNNNNE?*"

"Where's a dinosaur when you need one?" Alice groaned. Miss Goode stalked down the sidewalk and kicked her way through the shattered remains of the doorframe. Bob Craven turned and signaled a British officer tending to a wounded man.

"Arrest her! She's a traitor."

British Redcoats ran forward, advancing toward Miss Goode. Bob nudged the children. They grabbed the metal chest and started for the stairs in the commotion.

"I see you!" Miss Goode yelled. "You think you're going to get away from me? Give me those books!"

She swung the rifle on her shoulder, took aim and fired. The blast popped a chunk of brick from the wall near the staircase. The remaining British troops drew swords and circled Miss Goode.

"How dare you point those things at me?" Effigy Goode stormed as the officers advanced. "I own this store!"

"Drop that weapon," an office commanded. "Do it, madam, or we'll have you shot for sedition!"

"Is that so?" she snarled dropping her voice into a low and dangerous purr. "RUFUS!"

The dog leaped through the shattered window snarling. The British officers withdrew and some turned and ran into the back of the store. The dog's fangs dripped salvia as he barked and growled ferociously. He pounced on his front paws and raged with wild snarling. The wounded officers lay helpless, but the others ran through the doorway out into the streets or jumped through the broken window. Miss Goode stalked through the store and mounted the steps with an even gait.

Chapter Seven

Trapped!

Bob unlocked the door to Miss Goode's office and hurried the children and the chest inside. They all waited a long moment, their breathing hammering from their lips. They heard a key being turned in the lock.

"We've got to barricade the door," Jimmy yelled and they all ran to the desk. They pushed, but it was too heavy. Even with all of their weight, they could only scoot it a few inches. Walter grabbed a chair and slipped in under the knob and wedged the chair legs against the wooden floor. They all backed up toward the huge windows facing Main Street. The knob turned, but the door didn't open. The jiggling of the doorknob grew more frantic and then it stopped. Silence lingered for a few moments.

"What do we do?" Alice whispered. No one spoke. They all stared at each other in a daze. Jimmy looked over and met Walter's eyes.

"Do you know about this war?"

"Not really."

"I'm afraid I'm not up on my American history, either," Bob said. "I mean, being British and all."

Walter shook his head and stared down into the street where the fighting continued. "I think there are multiple battles going on all at the same time. The book must have been opened at several key spots."

"Robert?" a voice called from the other side of the door. Miss Goode sounded calm, almost pleasant.

"Yes?" Bob answered.

"Robert, we've known each other a long time. You've been a hard worker. I couldn't have asked for a more dedicated accountant. It's a lot of years to throw away, don't you think? Why you're helping those ragamuffins is somewhat of a mystery to me. Why don't you let me in? We'll all sit down and talk about it."

"I don't think that would be a very good idea," Bob said, trying to hide his nervousness, but his voice wavered.

"Robert, I was just frightened. All of this has got me rattled. I woke up from a sound sleep with Paul Revere riding a horse down my street screaming, 'the British are coming, the British are coming!' I brought my gun only for protection."

"Well, to be perfectly honest Effigy, you *did* shoot at us." Bob grimaced.

"I'll leave the gun outside when I come in."

"It's a trick," John shouted. "Don't believe her!"

"Is that my sweet little nephew?"

"Oh, now I *know* it's a trick," John hissed. Alice nodded.

"Look, Robert, the Revolutionary War went on for eight years. We need to stop it here and now. Rufus has them cornered, but we'll need the book to make it happen. You know that as well as I do. Give me the books and let me try to clean this up. Those dirty little children went snooping and look at the mess they've made."

"Is there another way out of here?" Jimmy asked. Bob's eyebrows inched together in concentration. He ran a hand through his white hair and readjusted his glasses. Finally he shook his head with a dismal frown.

"You can't stay in there forever!" Miss Goode yelled. Her voice turned shrill again. A blast from her rifle hit the door, but it held. All of them jumped. "I'm going to get in there and, when I do, I'll fix you all!"

They heard her reloading in the hallway. Bob grabbed Jimmy's arm and pulled him over to the side.

"We can climb out the window and inch along the ledge to the side of the building and then jump onto the roof of the undertaker's next door. That building is lower than this one. It's a good jump, though, ten feet at least."

"We wouldn't make it," Jimmy said, glancing around at everyone in the shadowy light of the room. "With all that mess going on outside, it's too dangerous. Somebody could fall or get shot."

"We could possibly use the ledge to get to the roof, but...."

"But there's no way to get down from there," Alice finished his thought.

"What a bloody mess!" Bob snapped. "We need to get her away from that door. If she would just clear the hallway, we could use the back staircase and get into the cellar again."

"I have an idea," Walter said. They all looked at him and he shrugged. "It's not a great idea or anything. I know our goal is to get all these things back into the books, but we have a trunk full. Couldn't we let something out? A diversion?"

"That's not bad." Jimmy laughed.

"Let's go for it," Tex nodded in agreement. "We got a crazy lady with a rifle, a war going on downstairs and dinosaurs in the alleys. Can't hurt."

Bob frowned.

"I'm not so sure. There's no way to be certain what would emerge out of those pages. It could be something...dangerous."

"OPEN THIS DOOR!!!" Effigy Goode screamed and another blast from her rifle echoed in the hallway. A chunk of wood sounded as if it had blown off with the shot.

"We better hurry," John said.

Tex let out a huff. "I don't know quite how to tell y'all this, but your aunt has gone a little looney."

"Get going, Walter," Alice yelled as she and Jimmy and Tex ran over and started piling chairs in front of the door. Walter and John dropped to the floor and threw the chest open. For a moment, some of the books seemed to quiver in anticipation of being opened. John put his hand on one and then snapped it away with an awful face. Walter prodded him with his elbow.

"What is it?"

"I think it *moved*," he hissed. He had felt something; a small electric current running over the leather cover. The books seemed to sizzle and pop. Walter scooped it up and read the title: *Frankenstein.*

"Nope, that would not be a good one. Let's keep looking."

Bob had jogged to the door and was trying to talk to Miss Goode, but she answered him with another crack of the rifle. He leaped back from the door. She reloaded again.

"The doors are not going to hold," Bob shouted, his voice going higher than normal. He fretted around the room looking for anything to pile in front of the door, but they had used almost everything. Walter began calling out titles to the books in a panic.

"Anything by Shakespeare? *Hamlet? King Lear?* Think something like that might work?"

"No," they all answered in unison.

"*The Scarlet Letter?*"

"No!"

"*Eldorado? Introduction to the Metaphysics of Morals?*"

"NO!"

"*Essays in Radical Empiricism?*"

"Oh for Pete's sake," Tex snarled.

"*The Canterbury Tales?*"

"That won't help us," Bob shouted, trying to remain calm, but his voice betrayed him. He used his handkerchief to wipe away the sweat from his brow.

"There are lots of poems. How about poetry?"

"We'll bore her to death," Jimmy muttered under his breath.

Walter gasped and everyone froze, turning to look at him in silence. Walter and John sat on the floor, staring at one of the leather-bound books. It was thinner than the others and Walter cradled it in his lap. He looked up with one eyebrow curled upward in triumph and smiled. John jumped from the floor and leaped two feet into the air with a shout. He clapped his hands and beamed. All of them ran over and read the poem's title, etched in gold across the leather case. Walter held it in his trembling fingers.

"Well, that might just do it," Bob said. The rifle exploded again, splintering the door near the knob.

———

Effigy Goode stood in the hallway with one ear pressed against the door. They had all gone quiet inside her office and that made her nervous. She knew there was nowhere for them to go but out the window, and it was a long drop to the street. *Maybe one of them will fall and snap a neck*, she thought and that brought a chuckle from deep within her.

"RUFUS!" she screamed and a moment later the huge dog leaped up the steps and came trotting down the long, dark hallway. She patted him twice on his massive head and then rubbed behind his ears. "Such a good boy! Did you teach those British twits a thing or two? Yes, you did. Now, when mommy gets the door open, remember...bite to *kill*!!"

She leveled the gun, braced it against her shoulder and pulled the trigger again. The sound echoed through the hallway and the wood around the doorknob gave way. She used the butt of the gun to hammer in the shattered wood. Her fingers curled inside and she felt the rim of the chair frame. She pressed against it and it slid back with lamps and chairs rattling along the floor.

"Here we go," she rumbled. The heavy oak doors flew back. Something snorted hot breath in Effigy Goode's face. She let out a shrill scream and stumbled back into the hallway. Her bedroom shoes, already wet from the snow outside, slipped on the hardwood floor and she came crashing down, landing hard on her scrawny backside. The rifle clattered to the floor. Shadows filled the doorway and long horns as big as the doorframe shifted in the shadowy light.

"Attack!" she screamed. Rufus growled, but didn't move. The sleek gray dog retreated two steps with a whine. Another huge snort blasted from a dark snout and Rufus turned tail and ran down the hallway.

"Come back here, Rufus!" Miss Goode demanded, but the dog had cleared the corner and his paws could be heard clatterring down the stairs. Rufus hurled himself through the doorway downstairs, ran straight down Main Street and was never seen again. A moment later the only sound was the soft jingling of small silver bells around the neck of the creature that blocked the doorway. Miss Goode shifted her gaze and then mustered all her courage.

"Whatever you are," she said, speaking slowly and trying not to let her nerves show, "I'm not to be trifled with around here."

"I feel the same way," a deep baritone said from the darkness. A chuckle of good humor escaped into the room and a golden light, so bright it hurt her eyes, exploded. Effigy Goode's mouth dropped open, her eyes staring unbelieving at the reindeer in the doorway. It snorted again, its massive antlers tilted to one side. She could see the room was filled with the furry creatures, all of them snorting and stomping their hooves on her Persian rug while golden trails of light twinkled on the furniture, the ceiling, the walls.

"What the—?" she started and then put her hands out beside her. She helped herself up from the floor and slid around the reindeer into the room. A gold-trimmed red sleigh almost twenty feet long sat perched on her desk with huge bundles of toys stuffed inside. Alice and John sat inside the sleigh, while Walter, Tex and Jimmy perched on top of the bags of toys, giggling, their heads only inches from the high ceiling. Bob Craven sat in the passenger's seat, the metal chest of books on the floor of the sleigh between his legs. On top of it lay an open leather book with the poem they had found inside. In gold letters neatly printed across the front it read, *A Visit from St. Nicholas.* Bob waved.

Effigy Goode ground her teeth.

Santa Claus held the reins in his hands. He was a round man, as expected, dressed in red velvet with an unusually long beard. It curled and dipped to the toes of his shiny, black boots. He chuckled and his rosy cheeks spread into a wide smile. Blue eyes, as deep and endless as the night sky, twinkled behind a pair of old spectacles.

"Well, well," Santa said shaking a finger of his black glove at Miss Goode. "I like to keep tabs and you haven't been very nice to these children, now have you?"

"I don't know if you can understand this, you jolly fat man," Miss Goode spat, "but you're only here because they released you! You're not real!"

"I have to disagree," he said. The reindeer became upset. They began stamping and snorting.

"Easy there, Dasher," Santa soothed. "I'm going to spirit these children away with me now—and unless you change those nasty ways, expect only coal in your stocking on Christmas morning."

"Oh, shut up!" she snapped. Her black eye slid over to

Alice and John. "You think you're both so smart, don't you? Well, I'll find you. I'll track you both down and, when I do, you'll wish you'd stayed on that Alabama farm. I won't spare you or your friends! And for you, Bob...well, you're fired, naturally."

"I assumed as much," he said with a courtly nod.

"But that's just the beginning. I'll put you somewhere nice and safe, out of the way of mischief. You know all too well that I can do it."

"Yes you can...but not tonight," he smiled and nodded toward Santa.

"We'll need to go through that window," Santa nodded and Effigy Goode watched as the glass began to dissipate. It faded until there was nothing there at all, only cold October wind rushing into her office.

"That was so *amazing*," Alice whispered under her breath, nudging her brother's arm. The reindeer stomped at the floor, trying to turn themselves around in the office. Some of them slammed into the walls, leaving holes in the ornate woodwork molding. Effigy Goode threw herself back out of the way as the reindeer got going, the jingling of the harness echoing. The sleigh shifted on the desk and the runners cut long scratches into the mahogany wood of the surface.

"That desk is priceless!" she screamed. The reindeer turned around until the sleigh faced the night outside. Miss Goode leaped back through the doorway and snagged her rifle. Santa adjusted his glasses and pulled a huge red velvet cloak up around him for warmth. Miss Goode charged back in the room and aimed the barrel at them. Santa chuckled.

"I wouldn't do that if I were you."

"Well, you're *not* me!" she yelled and fired. The rifle made an odd sound like a snort and a gurgle, and then gumdrops came plopping out the end. Santa sighed and shook his head wearily. He snapped the reins and Miss Goode staggered backward as the reindeer clicked their hooves and charged out the window, dragging the sleigh off the edge of the desk and into the wind. Its weight magically lifted as it became airborne. The sleigh and reindeer swooped through the window, leaving the smell of peppermint lingering in the room. They made a low dive toward Main Street and then banked to the left, curving upward on the wind currents. The sleigh lifted out of sight. Effigy stood by the wall, where only moments before glass windows had been, and felt the cold wind. Main Street was still alive with the Revolutionary War. In the distance, just on the cusp of a waxing moon that was almost full, she could see the reindeer and sleigh outlined. She could hear faintly in the distance, *"Happy Christmas to all and to all a good- night!"*

Effigy Goode threw her rifle across the room and screamed.

———

The park was alive with cannon fire. The dark tree line sheltered the two sides, firing at each other with pistols and muskets. Cannonballs hurled from the darkness across the grassy slopes. Jimmy hunkered down on the other side of a knoll and peered into the darkness. Walter crawled up beside him on his belly and poked his head through the grass.

"They're trying to take Bunker Hill," Walter whispered.

"Guess this is the place to be after all. We can thank Santa Claus for putting us down in the right spot."

"If we can get around this skirmish and into the camp, we can end all this before morning. Let's go. C'mon," Jimmy said, waving Tex, Bob, Alice and John along as they lowered their heads and ran through the trees. A cannonball hurtled overhead. They heard it crashing through the treetops, but didn't stop. Hopping over a patch of dirty snow, they rushed into the foliage of some bushes as the militia began firing on the Redcoats. Puffs of smoke popped through the branches.

"Get behind some trees," Tex yelled. Alice, John and Walter all slipped behind a large oak. Alice put her hands over John's ears as the cannons roared. Bob, Tex and Jimmy stepped forward into the darkness. The leather book lay open in Jimmy's hands.

"Excuse me, sir?" he yelled.

The Minuteman ran past Jimmy without stopping and became lost in the darkness. Another soldier halted a hundred feet away and inserted a paper cartridge of gunpowder into the barrel of his gun, using the ramrod to pack it down and then he was off running through the trees again.

"Pardon me?" Jimmy yelled, waving at a man in colonial clothing. The man's eyes trailed down Jimmy's clothing, looking obviously confused.

"Where are your weapons?"

"Can you look at this?" Jimmy asked, thrusting the book toward the Minuteman. The man turned his head and peered toward the pages with a huff. It was too dark to see anything. Bob nudged Jimmy.

"He has to touch it!"

"Are you some sort of British loyalists?" the Minuteman asked, fumbling for his pistol.

"We ain't British, we're Americans," Tex shouted with impatience. He reached out and grabbed the puffy white sleeve of the man's shirt. Tex dropped the man's left hand against the pages of the book and a blast of heat exploded into the night. A roaring sound, more ferocious than a tornado rumbled in their ears. Bob snagged Tex's collar, jerking him backward as a wave of white light soared across the park. The heat was intense. Jimmy, Tex and Bob fell to the ground, temporarily blinded by the light that covered everything around them. A moment later, it was over. Jimmy blinked away the bluish glow from his vision and found himself sprawled on the wet ground in the forest. Tex sat up and shook his head. Bob crawled on all fours and stood up, rocking on his feet. Alice was at his side in an instant, supporting him. Walter and John came running over helping Jimmy and Tex up. The last of the snow was gone, melted in the heat that had flooded from inside the book.

"At least we didn't get shot," Tex grumbled as Alice scooped up the leather book and snapped the buckle, tugging on the strap until it was tight.

The hobo jungle was crowded with people as Tex, Walter and John entered the firelight. Jimmy, Alice and Bob brought up the rear, still talking enthusiastically about their conquest as people moved around them in the darkness. A Union Pacific Big Boy was sitting dead on the tracks, the engine cold. Old Willie gave a laugh and shout when he saw them. Jimmy ran over and gave him a hearty handshake and then introduced Bob. He turned with an outstretched hand toward Alice and John, but Old Willie just pushed Jimmy aside.

"You don't need to introduce these two," he laughed, grabbing them both up in his gigantic arms for a barrel hug. "They brought me this here coat I'm wearing."

"Everyone here okay?" Alice asked and Willie shrugged.

"We had some Redcoats come 'round trying to boss us outta here. Those blasted Redcoats tried to take our jungle under siege. We brought out some firepower of our own, a little dynamite Wilbur scored from when he was on a blasting crew up north. They turned tail and run over yonder beyond the tracks and set up camp. Those cannons been going for hours, but about five minutes ago everything went still. Nothing but dead quiet."

"So...you know what was happening?" Walter asked and Willie grinned, scratching his beard.

"The Revolutionary War? It don't take a genius to work it out. I read about it once in a history book."

"You handled it better than the folks in town," Tex snorted. "Main Street won't be the same for awhile."

"I've seen stranger things," Willie said. "We've got some stew brewing and Jeb caught a mess of chickens on the outskirts of town. It's good eatin's for the whole camp."

"Can we stay the night?" Jimmy asked. Willie threw back his head and howled like a wolf. He raised his hands in to the sky.

"You betcha!" he bellowed.

After eating as much chicken as they could stomach,

they all gathered around a fire and talked. The flames jumped from the logs, casting orange shadows over their faces. The night was cold and the fire felt good. John fell asleep propped against Alice's knees. His head flopped to one side.

Jimmy returned from another part of the camp and eased himself down on a stump. "Well, that train is sitting there 'cause nothing can get in or out of Carson Corners. The lake has risen and covered part of the tracks farther north. They think it has to do with all the snow affecting the water level, but somehow I doubt it."

"What do you think happened?" Alice asked in a soft voice, so as not to wake John.

"If I had to guess," he said, rubbing the back of his neck with his hand, "I'd say the copy of *Moby Dick* was open too long."

"Oh great, merciful Jehoshaphat!" Tex grumbled, slapping his hand on his leg. "That's the last thing we need. Just got rid of a blasted war and now you're telling me we gotta get a whale back in a little book?"

"I could be wrong," Jimmy sighed, "but those old timers were talking about how all the bass and trout were floating along the banks."

"Why?" Bob asked.

"Salt water," Jimmy said with his eyebrows lifting. "They say the lake is turning to salt water. It's killing all the fish."

"Why else would a natural-fed lake suddenly be filling with salt water unless it's turning into an ocean?" Walter questioned out loud, his eyes staring into the flames.

"Moby Dick was larger than a normal whale," Bob began.

"Most sperm whales grow to be fifty, maybe sixty feet long, and if he's bigger than that it's going to take time to figure out how to deal with this issue. The water level will have to rise considerably to be able to support a mammal that large."

"How are we ever going to get all these things back in?" Walter asked.

Bob cleaned his glasses on his coat. "Remember, only one Minuteman had to touch that book and everything associated with the Revolutionary War disappeared. It affects them all."

"But not the damage."

"No," Bob agreed. "You're right about that."

Alice dropped her voice into a low whisper. "I don't want John involved in this anymore. He's too young. Something bad might happen. I need to get him away from all this for a while. Isn't there someplace he could go? Somewhere safe from Effigy Goode?"

"Speaking of Miss Goode," Jimmy interupted, "when we were back in the store, she said something kinda odd. She said she'd put you away somewhere, Bob. She said something about you knowing she could do it. What did she mean?"

"You know what's been happening," Walter said. "You knew about the books."

Bob paused for a long moment and then looked away from their steady stares. The firelight danced and a log shifted, popping. A shower of small sparks floated into the dark sky and got caught in the wind. The sparks burned out and drifted away. Bob breathed a sigh of relief and shrugged.

"I would have told you eventually, but there hasn't been

time to sit down and talk it through. I'm not really Bob Craven. My name is Bob Cratchit."

"From *A Christmas Carol?*" Walter questioned with his eyes growing wide.

"That's right. I told you I was a fan of Charles Dickens. Miss Goode pulled me out of the book a long time ago. She did that for many of the employees that have worked for her over the years. They were given cheap room and board, minimal wages and promised they could go back into the pages of their lives someday as long as they obeyed her."

"Hold up here," Tex interrupted. "You're telling us you're not real? You're like those Redcoats and Minutemen?"

"No, I'm very real. I'm as real as you or Alice or Jimmy. I'm as real as anyone, but *only* because I've been ripped from the written page into this world. Anne Simmons for example, one of the ladies who works in the store, she's really *Anne of Green Gables*. Huck Flannery who loads the stock from the trucks and checks everything into inventory? He's really *Huckleberry Finn* all grown up. Here in this world, we age and change like everyone else. We've been here for years."

"Holy cow," Tex shouted. "I must be dumber than dirt 'cause this is just now sinking in! You're out of that book with Mr. Scrooge, right?"

"Yes," Bob chuckled. "Although Ebenezer Scrooge has nothing on Miss Goode. She's a horrid, odious woman."

"How could you work for her all these years?" Alice asked, running her fingers through John's soft blond hair while he slept.

"It hasn't been that bad," he said with a smile. "I borrowed *A Christmas Carol* from the library and read it almost at once. That was around 1906. I know what happens. My son, Tim, doesn't die because Mr. Scrooge is visited by the three ghosts and everything changes. Our lives all turn out just fine. Knowing that has been a great comfort to me. I didn't feel the need to rush back to the pages of the book, not to the Christmas of 1843. I knew everything would be all right, but I still hope someday to get back there. I miss my wife and my children and Camden Town, but the life I've had here has been a good one. I've seen the invention of airplanes and cars and things I never would have dreamed. Besides, if I go back someday, I'll be the same age that I was when I left. Inside those pages, you only know a limited amount of time and space."

"So all these years you've lived in fear of Miss Goode?" Alice asked.

"Yes...total, absolute fear. She's a dangerous woman. If I ever want to get back, she's the only way to do it. Granted, some of the characters she forced out years ago, they know what happens to them and some of them are happy never to return to the printed page. Those people live in fear of her sending them back, while others have to do whatever she says to get home. If she decided to burn the books, I'd never be able to get back."

"You really dropped a ton of bricks with this one," Tex said, whistling softly. "I can't believe it. You came out of a book."

"I think we're all caught up on that," Walter said, rolling his eyes. Tex snorted.

"Well, excuse me! All I'm saying is that it's pretty far out there."

"Where's the copy of *A Christmas Carol?*" Jimmy asked. All of them turned toward Bob with eager eyes.

"No one knows. Miss Goode hid the books a long time ago and has threatened us almost weekly so we'd never forget the power she has over us. When I saw you had unearthed that chest, I was scared, elated, and nervous. I thought maybe at last someone had found them and we could go home."

"So," Jimmy began, taking a deep breath, "if she means what she said tonight, she'll never let you go back into the book?"

"That's right," Bob nodded with a sad smile. His blue eyes reflected the fire's light through his glasses. Everyone sat in silence for a while. Bob finally broke the firelight's spell. "I have to admit that, after helping you all tonight, I'm keen to see my children again. I think I'd forgotten just how much I missed them until I spent time around all of you. But if it's not to be, then I'll live out my life here in Carson Corners or somewhere else. One way or another, we'll try to get everything back in order. Still though...what I wouldn't give to go down a slide in Cornhill at the end of a lane of boys just once more on Christmas Eve."

"Bob, you're welcome to stay with us for as long as..." Alice said, her words floating off into silence. She cleared her throat and started again. "You can stay with us no matter what. John and I can't really go home and we sure can't go back to Aunt Effigy."

"Don't worry," Jimmy smiled. "We'll all be okay. We'll stick together."

Sometime later, Alice lay curled on her side, her eyes

open while the fire slowly died. Everyone else was fast asleep. She had her arm looped over her brother's shoulder. Tex was snoring. Walter was asleep on his stomach, his face pressed into his outstretched arms, mouth hanging open. Bob was flat on his back, his face tranquil in sleep. *I wonder if he's dreaming of his home or where he grew up,* Alice thought. She shifted and crawled over to Jimmy and woke him up. They whispered together for a few moments and then left the dying embers of the fire together. They knocked on Old Willie's door and he grumbled, "Come in."

Alice and Jimmy found him sitting up in the middle of his bed roll, his hair curly and standing up from his head in tangles. They sat on the cold floor inside his shack.

"We need some help," Alice began. Old Willie sat sleepy-eyed, smacking his lips until the weight of her story hit him. A few moments later, he was wide awake. The pale glow of fireflies inside a glass jar by his bedroll provided a strange, golden light inside the wood and metal shack. Old Willie listened intently. He broke out a piece of fish bone he used as a needle and mended his worn pair of shoes, darning the heel back to the sole.

"What do you think?" Jimmy asked after Alice had finished. The flat, cold gray of early morning hung in the air with a misty chill. Outside the shack, the camp came to life with the sounds of chattering voices, pots and pans clanking together and singing. Willie rolled his lips inward and then out, pursing them together with a smack. He nodded.

"We'll help anyway we can."

Alice felt so happy she could cry. She turned her face away from them, looking at the jar sitting by the bed and tapping on the glass so Willie and Jimmy wouldn't see the tears forming in her eyes. The largest bug she'd ever seen flew inside, darting and moving so fast that it was blurry. The body was dark, wrapped in a patchwork of tiny, torn leaves. The wings beat so fast it reminded her of a hummingbird. When she saw the dark eyes through the luminescent glow she gasped.

"Ain't that the sweetest firefly you ever seen?" Willie howled. "Found it down in the weeds a night or two back. Big as a hornet and just about as ornery too."

Alice gulped and then tried to offer a thin smile. "Old Willie, that's not a firefly. It's Tinkerbell."

Chapter Eight

A Whale's Tale and the Hobo Dino Patrol

"We've scouted out Carson Lake," Jimmy announced, returning from a morning walk with Tex and Bob. A plank of wood lay warped and decaying in the sunlight on the slats of two chairs. Alice used it as a desk while she sat propped on a rock. A crowd of hobos stood around, mumbling to each other while sipping coffee from battered tin cups. Walter sat beside her with John squeezed in between them, hovering over a map. Old Willie stood nearby, a hand on his hip and his face unreadable, but Jimmy thought he saw a tinge of unease. There was a strange current in the air; everyone was excited, unsettled, hopeful.

"How does it look?" Walter asked and everyone moved their eyes from the map of Carson Corners stretched out on the makeshift desk and looked at Jimmy.

"It's gettin' bigger by the minute."

"All salt water now," Bob reported, wiping beads of sweat from his forehead. He eased himself down on a log and took a ladle from a water bucket. He drank and then sighed with a bitter frown. "Not like having a good cup of tea, is it?"

"We couldn't get close," Tex said, removing his hat and fanning himself. "Darned thing has spread up and out."

"It's into the next county and heading this way," Jimmy said. "If we don't stop it soon, it's going to cover Carson Corners, Newberry and Charlotte."

"And on and on," Tex finished, spitting into the high weeds. "There ain't gonna be a North Carolina pretty soon if we don't grease our wheels and move quick as lightening. Can you picture it? An ocean swallowing everything in its path: Georgia, Alabama, Mississippi, Louisiana, Texas. A whale swimming happy as can be through every town and city between here and God-knows-where. And all of it buried under water."

"Wait a minute," Alice said looking down at the map, which had four large rocks anchoring the corners. She ran her fingers along the county lines and then looked at Jimmy. "You said the next county was already flooding?"

"We passed some folks on the road that told us they were starting to evacuate over there."

"You're wrong, Tex," Alice said, drawing her finger across the map's boundaries. "It won't move westward. It doesn't need to. The water will rise and spread out as it goes *east*. When it connects to the Atlantic, the whale will swim out to sea."

"And we'll be sunk," John added.

"We have to stop him before that," Jimmy growled. "The

whole eastern part of the state would be submerged."

Tex continued. "We could see the top of Newberry Hill in Anders County, but it was almost under water. No sign of the whale yet."

"It won't be long," Walter said. "If it's gotten that deep the whale will be visible soon. He has to come up for air."

"We've got some men working on harpoons," Alice grinned. "We'll have weapons by early afternoon, right Willie?"

"Anything you say, missy." He waved and chuckled. "These folks around here are a little curious and a bit cautious, but we didn't have much trouble convincing them of what's happening, especially after they saw the war break out last night."

A man in a thin coat, his collar ragged and trailing black thread, spoke up. His eyes were dark and his hair was slicked back from his high forehead. "I hate to say it, but ain't no one gonna stop that whale. I read that book years ago and it sank Ahab's ship. It went down in a funnel of water, sucked to the bottom of the sea. I don't rightly know what's going on in this wacky town, but one thing I do know—you kids are not going to be able to bring down the white whale with some homemade harpoons!"

Some of the other men and women nearby nodded in agreement. A baby started crying somewhere in the camp. Rumblings of conversation erupted. Alice looked at Jimmy and then winked at him. She held up her hands and stood up. "Look, I know all of this is confusing, but we don't have to kill the whale. We've got to get the copy of *Moby Dick* close enough to touch him and, considering he's as long as that train sitting over there, it won't be easy. We thought we could attach the book to the harpoon and get him that way "

"How you gonna get close enough?" another man asked.

"We have a way," Alice grinned. "We'll be able to get right up next to him."

A group of men came forward from the shantytown and the crowd parted to make way. A redheaded young man with a scruffy fedora took center stage. He nodded at Alice and then spoke in a clear, strong voice.

"Ma'am, we're all loaded up and ready to go."

"Thanks, Newton." She smiled.

"It's our Hobo Dino Patrol." Tex giggled.

"Okay," Alice announced, pitching her voice out over the crowds. Everyone sank into silence as Alice's voice sang out clear in the crisp morning air. "Newton Graham is going to lead a group of men into the woods and see if they can get a line on the—" Alice glanced at Walter with a frown. "What's it called?"

"Tyrannosaurus Rex."

"Right!" she agreed. "They'll be trying to bait a trap for him somewhere between the alley we saw him in last night and Withers Park. There might be other dinosaurs loose, but we've only seen one and some of Newton's group found droppings in the alley leading toward the woods. That's where they'll search first. Newton, if you find a dinosaur, *any* dinosaur, try to get the book in close range. If the pages touch one of them, it will take them *all* back inside. Jimmy, Tex and I are going to stay and make sure the weapons are secured...and then take on the whale."

"If we can find 'im," Tex muttered under his breath.

Jimmy leaned over, whispering. "Something that big

might find us before we're ready to find him."

"Old Willie and some of the other men are going into town and check out *Goode's Mercantile.* They'll be keeping close tabs on Miss Goode at her house on Morton Hill too. We can't let her try to skip town or anything like that until we have all the books safely back with us." She looked over at Bob and he was beaming. His eyes sparkled in the morning light.

"Nobody knows where she hid those books?" Old Willie questioned. Alice shook her head.

"No, and there's no telling what she might do with them. She could burn them or open them up and let who-knows-what out into the world. She's got to be contained at all costs."

"I think Alice missed her calling," Walter commented to Jimmy. "She should have been a general."

"Questions?" Alice asked.

"What about me?" John asked in a small voice.

"Bob and Walter are taking you into town."

"Why?"

"Because it's too dangerous," she snapped.

"I want to stay!"

"No," she growled. "That's it, everyone, and thank you so much for your help!"

Alice sat down. John had tears in his eyes. As the crowd started to disperse, she draped an arm around him. "I'm sorry, John. I don't want anything to happen to you. The things we're doing are dangerous. Somebody could get hurt."

"What about you? What if something happens?" he blubbered.

"That's why we've got Walter and Bob staying with you You're going to the Salvation Army and wait until we've got a handle on some of this. It won't be for long."

He nodded as tears streamed down his face. Walter and Bob gathered themselves up and John took Walter's hand in his with a frown. As they started to walk away, he ran back and hugged Jimmy, Alice and Tex.

"Everything will be okay." Alice smiled, but inside she was worried. All it would take was one slip, one moment where they weren't paying attention, one second when something bad could happen. She waved as the three of them walked through the rows of shacks and vanished in the tall weeds over the hill.

———

Alice walked with Tex and Jimmy to a grassy hill just above the railroad depot and looked over the tops of the trees at Carson Lake. The water level had risen even higher in the last few hours. The clouds hid the sun, but thin shafts of light broke free, falling on the surface of the water. A flock of seagulls squawked overhead and vanished in the glare of clouds only to reappear over the waves, which had started crashing against the shoreline.

"It's kinda pretty," Alice said. "We're watching an ocean being made. Makes me think what it must be like to see the world being born."

"If y'all need a moment alone, let me know," Tex grumbled. Alice and Jimmy both looked at him with sour faces. Tex shrugged. "I didn't know if you wanted to go collect seashells or smooch or recite poetry or something."

Old Willie came panting over the hill with a few of the hobos from the jungle following. Hoisted over their shoulders were harpoons made from wooden shafts and rope. The harpoons had been whittled to sharp points.

"So, that's Carson *Ocean*," Willie chuckled as the clouds parted and the sun reflected on the choppy surface of the water. A second later, a white mountain appeared from beneath the waves and blew a stream of water a hundred feet into the air. The water exploded with a hiss like steam being released.

"Wow," Jimmy said under his breath. They saw the whale dip back into the waves and the tail came sliding to the surface as big as a four-story building. It slapped the water with a splash, sending a rain shower into the sky, and then it was gone.

"Never seen anythin' like that in my life," Tex said in awe. Old Willie put a hand on Tex's shoulder.

"Are you sure you're up to this-here mess? It won't be pretty."

"We've got to do it," Tex said as stoic as a rock.

"Piece of cake." Jimmy laughed and Alice tried to smile, but she felt nauseated.

"Okay, let's go," she said. Alice, Tex and Jimmy secured the rope around their waists and made sure the harpoons were strapped along their backs. They checked to make sure the book was safe with Alice. She had it tucked inside the folds of her overalls and secured with a belt. Old Willie looked them up and down and then popped his finger in his mouth. He sucked twice and then pulled it free and aimed it into the air.

"Good southern wind." He laughed and knew there was no point delaying any longer. He clapped them all on the heads, giving them the traditional hobo blessing: "By rail or by road, blue skies or storm, good Lord deliver us."

Willie reached into the massive pocket of his coat and withdrew the glass jar. He held it over Jimmy's head and gave a big grin. He shook the jar. The holes he punched in the top made a kind of saltshaker. Tinkerbell was jumbled against the glass, but soft wispy trails of golden light sifted out the top and fell over Jimmy's hair.

"It tickles," he laughed. Willie did the same to Alice and then to Tex.

"What now?" Jimmy asked.

"Think happy thoughts." She shrugged.

Willie tapped the side of the glass jar and then jumped. "She's mad as a viper." He sang a few bars of an Irish folk song in a soothing voice, then slipped the jar back into his pocket.

"Any luck?" Tex asked.

"She's not going to calm down anytime soon." Old Willie grinned.

"I don't think this is working," Jimmy said. Old Willie's mouth dropped open and his eyes grew to the size of saucers. "What?" Jimmy asked and Willie pointed to the grassy earth. Jimmy looked down and realized he wasn't touching the ground. His feet dangled a few inches above the grass.

Alice made a weird sound in her throat and they all looked over to find her levitating into the air. She had floated a good ten feet from the hillside when Tex let out a whoop and lifted like a balloon into the blue sky. Jimmy, still floating, looked down to tell Old Willie that it was great, better than he ever thought possible, but Old Willie was a good twenty feet below him.

"Move your arms!" Alice called and Jimmy found if he parted the air like doing a breast stroke in water, he could propel himself forward. They all began to move out away from the hill and over the treetops. Jimmy cast a quick look back and saw the group of hobos in the distance, waving. Old Willie's face was no bigger than a penny. They all soared out over the hills, looking at the tiny farms and fields below them. Jimmy steadied himself when a gust of wind hit and he started to lose his balance. He dipped below the wind current and settled into a nice even pace. The air smelled clean and fresh, and the wind moved through his hair and his clothes, his shirt flapping in the cold breeze.

"I LOVE ITTTTTTTTTT!" Tex shouted and Jimmy saw his friend was a long way to his right, maybe a hundred feet, doing cartwheels in the air. He watched Tex skip and soar through a patch of low-hanging clouds and then Jimmy couldn't help himself. He started laughing. He threw back his head and laughed and yelled and pushed with his body until he was zipping through the late afternoon sky faster than he ever dreamed.

It's amazing, Alice thought. Her arms were straight out beside her and her body seemed to float on a cushion of air. She looked down and they were over the water now. White foam topped the waves. To her left, a flock of birds came flapping along and she watched them watch her. *What must they think of us?* she questioned. *Do they know what we are or do we just look like three strange birds flapping along in their sky and riding the tail wind with them?*

Alice saw Jimmy begin to do a zigzag pattern. As his body moved, she watched the air currents shift with him and a small trail of golden light followed in his wake. *It's the fairy dust,* she thought and arched her back, sailing upward into the massive blue dome of the sky.

"LOOK!" Jimmy yelled. Alice heard his voice only because it caught the wind and came singing to her ears. She looked down. Jimmy hovered in the sky, pointing toward a white island in the middle of the water. It took Alice a moment to realize it was the whale. He had surfaced. She dropped down, moving through the air, and caught up to Jimmy. He reached out a hand and their fingers touched. She felt how cold his fingers were, but with their hands locked they didn't float away from each other. She looked at him and laughed. His face was red and chilled from the October air and his hair was a mess. Alice held tight to his coat collar and looked down at the whale. They were only a few hundred feet above him and she could see the dark shadows of lances and harpoons buried in the great snowy hump of the whale's back.

"Now's our chance," Jimmy yelled over a strong breeze that came out of the south. Alice nodded and then she looked around, something catching her attention. She heard something wailing in the wind like the cry of some strange bird, but the skies were empty except for fat, cumulus clouds like marshmallow mountains.

"Where's Tex?" she shouted. Alice and Jimmy scanned the horizon and saw him dancing over clouds in the far distance. They called to him, but he didn't hear. "It doesn't matter, I've got the book."

Alice reached into her belt and touched the soft, faded leather of the book and then stopped. The same sound she'd heard before echoed in the sky. She looked around and saw Jimmy's eyes were growing wide.

"Do you hear that? What is it?" she asked. He hooked an arm under her elbow and spun her around in midair. A dark, winged shape emerged from the north and flapped its way toward them. The wingspan was at least twenty-five feet and the sharp beak turned on a strange pointed head. It let out another shriek that made the air tremble.

"DIVE!" Jimmy yelled. He snagged the back of her shirt and dragged her with him toward the surface of the water. They lost all the grace of flying as Jimmy sped like a bullet toward Carson Lake with Alice in tow. Alice tried to get her balance, but there was nothing to hold on to for support. Her legs and arms flailed wildly in the wind as Jimmy held on tight. The creature saw them dropping for the waves and started a simultaneous descent to catch them before they could hit the water. The long snout opened and rows of tiny sharp teeth caught the light. The ferocious wind froze on Alice's face. The water rushed up to greet them and they hit with a tremendous splash. Darkness swirled around Alice for what seemed like years. The next thing she knew, the sky was above her and Jimmy was supporting her as they floated in the water. Alice spat salt water through her lips and looked around.

"What happened?"

"Some kind of flying dinosaur," Jimmy said, coughing. "It came out of nowhere. It almost got us. I was too scared to look, but I felt its shadow as we hit."

"I can't seem to fly," Alice groaned, attempting to lift herself from the waves. She floundered in the water and Jimmy shook his head.

"I've already tried. It's no use. Maybe when we get wet it washes the magic off or something. I don't know."

"How far are we from shore?"

"I think if we start swimming, we could be in by nightfall."

Alice looked up. "What happened to Tex?"

"I'm not sure, but...there he is!" Jimmy shouted. They could see him curving through the air. His body was a dark spot in the blue; coming up fast on his heels was the same dinosaur that had attacked them. The dark, gray body was sleek and leathery, and the wings flapped like thunder as it lunged through the late afternoon sky.

"Oh God," Alice said, grabbing Jimmy's arm. "It's going to get him."

"He'll have to make land or hit the water."

The winged creature dipped and rode the air with the ease only millions of years of evolution could give it, the giant stalk of a beak thirty feet behind Tex and closing. The boy flew as fast as he could. His arms kicked at the wind. He banked to the right, soared through some low cloud cover and exploded from the cloud with trails of it dragging from his boots. He headed their way. Alice could see in his tiny face the terror that had already swelled in her heart. He was *never* going to make it.

———

Newton Graham was seventeen and had been riding the rails for over a year. His father, Nathaniel Graham, was a preacher out of Redbone, Mississippi. Newton had spent more time in a church pew than he cared to remember. When Newton was only knee high to a grasshopper he was as solid a fixture in church as the alter itself. His father would climb in the pulpit on Sunday mornings and start out nice and easy—a few Bible quotes, some hymns, prayers for the needy—but it was all a prelude to a religious explosion. There was always the moment when his father would pull out a handkerchief and start to mop away the sweat from his bald head. Newton knew his father had finished warming up and was ready to make some noise. That handkerchief was a white flag of surrender to the Holy Ghost. Newton's dad might as well have been calling his shot by pointing to center field, just like the Bambino in the '32 World Series. The handkerchief didn't go back into his father's breast pocket until the service was over. His dad would wave it around and throw back his head, hollering like a madman when the gospel filled him.

Now, Newton didn't know what a dinosaur looked like, outside of some picture books he'd seen once, but he was pretty sure there was no scripture to recite when hunting one down. The dinosaurs didn't look bad as he remembered—bright green like lizards, only bigger. He was sure they could handle it, but a part of him wished his father were there next to him. He felt sure his father could talk a dinosaur back into a book, save the thing's scaly soul and form a sing-along of *Shall We Gather by the River* in two seconds flat.

Newton eased his group of men through the woods, following some dinosaur tracks in the last remains of snow. The prints were a good size and deep, which meant the thing must be hefty. Newton had hunted deer and squirrel for supper, but this was the first time he was looking for something that might eat *him*. They had tracked the critter's prints from town and now they were deep in Withers Woods. Swallowing the fear in his throat, he used hand signals to bring his second flank forward in the thick underbrush. He touched the leather book Alice had given him inside his coat's pocket and felt a shiver. At first, he thought it had to do with the chill of being so deep in the forest and the lack of sunlight through the thick overhead branches, but then he realized it was something else.

Something was wrong. No birds were singing in the trees. There wasn't a crack of twig disturbing the woods, not a scattering of pine needles caught in a breeze, not a whisper of wind except for his own breath ringing in his ears.

"Somethin's about to happen," he hissed. Jonah Morgan stopped at his side, glancing all around him, but the forest was as silent as a bone yard. He waited. Listening to the empty forest, Newton was certain of only one thing: they were stalking something or something was stalking them. Easing himself down, he picked up a branch as tall as he was and heaved it from behind the tree into a grassy clearing. Nothing. He shrugged and signaled his group to move forward. Two steps later, the tree limbs scattered and a roar echoed through the hills. Newton threw himself back behind the tree with a shout and the other hobos dove into the underbrush. The Tyrannosaurus Rex snorted and brought his blocky head down. The teeth hit the branch Newton had thrown and the wood splintered apart on impact.

Jonah was squeezed against Newton's shoulder, looking over with sweat on his cheeks and his eyes glazed in fear. "Now what?" Jonah whispered.

Newton thought for a long moment and then pulled the leather book from his coat. He unbuckled the strap and threw open the tattered pages. "Only one thing to do," he said. He'd seen his daddy preach at least two thousand sermons. He knew what his father would do. Newton jumped from behind the tree and stood in the clearing. He froze. Newton wasn't sure the thing could see him when he was still. The head was moving left and right as if trying to detect something in his field of vision. Newton held the book up high and shouted at the top of his lungs.

"GET YOU BEHIND ME, OLD DEVIL!"

The creature saw him raise the book and charged. Newton pitched the book on the wind, throwing it at the dinosaur that lumbered toward him, making the earth tremble with the muscles of its legs. The leather gave some weight to the book somewhat so it had a nice arch. The pages fluttered in the wind, but it hit the dinosaur on the snout. A streak of white light burned through the forest. Newton closed his eyes, ready to be devoured, but a heat as strong as he'd ever felt knocked him flat. When he opened his eyes, Jonah Morgan was standing over him. The other fellas came forward and one gave a soft whistle.

"Never seen anyone try to cast out a dragon."

Newton shrugged, grinned and passed out.

———

Alice screamed. The beak of the monster curved like a sickle in the sky as it approached Tex from behind, the wings arching out stiff on a tail wind. The black eyes were shiny like an oil slick as it lurched forward. The winged beast closed the gap and opened its jaws to snag Tex...and was gone. A light so radiant filled the sky that Alice thought the sun had emerged from some clouds at just the right angle and blinded her momentarily. She blinked. Tiny bubbles of light faded from her eyes and the flying dinosaur was truly gone. Tex was still scrambling for his life, unaware of the change. He flapped his arms and legs through the air, and they could hear him yelling.

"Who-hooooooooooo!" Jimmy yelled. Alice laughed and waved. Tex zipped above them, spiraling down toward the treetops a few miles off in the distance. Only the tops of the tallest trees were still above water. Tex sailed into a wall of pine and elm and disappeared, leaving broken branches in his wake.

"How long do you think it'll take him to realize he's not supper?" she asked. Jimmy shrugged.

"I hope he's okay. He hit that tree line pretty hard."

"He's bound to be...what? Three, four miles from here?"

"At least."

The water had grown calm and still. Alice's legs were tired of kicking. She looked out across the water and had trouble seeing the grassy hill they had started from when first taking flight. She realized with growing concern it could have been twenty miles away—or fifty? She glanced around and realized how far out into the middle of nowhere they were. Only water and sky to the north as far as the eye could see. To the south a small bit of land was highlighted against the horizon. To the east there were some trees and a tiny ridge. Tex had landed somewhere in the west, where the sun was starting to sink.

Seagulls swarmed the water's surface and Alice looked at Jimmy. Both of them were coated in dying sunlight, the water turning red with the day's last few rays. They both wore the same expression of fear. Then the water tingled under Alice's feet and everything exploded around them. The sheer force of the waves shook Jimmy away from Alice and sent him flying, in a cloud of foam and salt water, three hundred feet away. Alice wiped her face and realized she was riding the top of a wave. The flow of the current was pushing her farther out to sea. She floated on the crest, helpless, and saw in horror that Moby Dick had surfaced.

———

Bob was sitting with John and Walter in the Salvation Army's main dining hall. The place overflowed with people. Some had come from farther out in the county, trying to escape the rising water, others had their homes damaged during the Revolutionary War, and still others were just hobos looking for a clean place to sleep. Since the trains had stopped running due to snow and the rising waters of Carson Lake, the hobos had been unable to catch out. Despite the cheerful Halloween decorations dotting the walls, a feeling of disquiet and unrest rumbled through the hall. Bob had gotten some food for them and they all sat together at the end of a table. John only picked at his food, but Walter stuffed a slice of cornbread down and munched on an apple. Voices swelled around them.

"It's dark outside," John said, glancing through the long, thin windows set back in the block walls. Walter and Bob looked up. John played with the spoon in his soup bowl.

"No need to worry, little man. They'll be fine," Bob said. "They know we're here and safe and that's one less thing they have to worry about. You should eat up, John."

"I'm not hungry," he said as Walter cupped his bowl to his lips and tilted his head back. He drained the last of the tomato soup. Walter wiped the sleeve of his coat across his mouth and sighed.

"That was tasty."

"Not bad indeed." Bob chuckled.

Walter looked embarrassed and then nodded. "Guess it won't hurt to ask if I can have some more, huh?"

"You can have mine," John said, sliding the bowl across the table.

Walter shoved it back.

"No. Eat up, Big John. You've got to keep up your strength. I'm gonna go to the outhouse. Be back in a sec."

Walter hopped from his place and walked through the mass of people. He cleared the side hall and peered into the kitchen. Steam lifted from pots on the stove while volunteers in white aprons moved through the smoky haze. Walter ducked out the door into the cold night air and worried about Jimmy, Alice and Tex. It had been hours since they'd left them at the hobo jungle. They had promised they would be back in town by nightfall, even if they didn't manage to get the whale back in the book. The last glow of daylight still lingered beyond the bare treetops in town. An icy wind had picked up. Walter walked down the steps, stepped off the path into the grass and never made it to the outhouse. A dark shape sprang from out of the cold twilight and seized him by the throat.

———

Alice watched as the last light of day streamed across the whale's white backside. The breaching mammal rode through the water, sending waves a mile wide in its wake. The whale circled off to the left and she could see the glimmer of an eye watching her as it swam on, cutting a wider and wider path around her. She could feel her feet kicking frantically, but the whale was moving at super speeds and a vortex was forming both under and around her.

"JIMMY!" she screamed, but her voice seemed to go dead the moment it hit the air. The waves crashed around her, blocking out the sound of her voice. Night was fast approaching and the ghostly white whale swam a few hundred feet to her side in slow, rhythmic motions. A cold twinkle of starlight floated overhead. *It's trying to drag me under*, she thought and felt the pressure of the vortex building as the whale came back for another spin. It swam closer this time, the waves knocking against her as she was tossed back and forth. The water made a sucking sound and began to hollow out around her.

A shadow zipped overhead and Alice shut her eyes, afraid some new horror had found her. Watching the whale from the corner of her eye, she shot a hard glance up and found Tex not more than ten feet above her, floating on the wind. She thought he was shouting something, but she couldn't hear him. He stretched out his hand and she reached up, clutching his wrist. Tex pulled with all his might and Alice popped free from the water, her feet dripping into the cold sea. The wind hit her full force and froze her clothing to her skin.

Moby Dick stopped circling and slid off into the darkness, his tail smacking at the water. The vortex began to die out and the choppy waves relaxed. Tex struggled to hold Alice up and keep himself from sinking as well. He was trying to go higher, but only seemed to get about fifteen feet from the water's surface before starting to dip back down. Unable to use his hands to fly, he could just barely keep them floating across the surface of the dark water. Alice heard the water breaking and saw the whale shoot up from the depths, its slick white bulk moving against the night sky, and then crash back into the water to her right. A blast from the blowhole in the front of its enormous head sent a geyser of water into the air. Now the whale's head was just under the surface, a white battering ram coming toward them at full speed.

"Hold onto me!" she shouted. Tex held tight with both hands.

Alice fumbled in her belt and pulled the book free with one hand. The whale could easily take her and Tex into his mighty jaws and crush them in one bite—or drag them down in its wake and drown them. Tex's fingers were crushing the wrist of her left hand. Alice held the wet book in her hands, the pages rustling in the October wind.

The whale was only a few hundred feet to their left and closing the gap faster than she could have imagined even in her dreams. It looked like a train, all fleshy and white, rumbling through the water. The head emerged like a stone wall, pocked and scarred with age and the harpoon lances. She threw the book, praying silently it would hit somewhere. The pages fluttered like a white bird in the dark as it sailed toward the whale. The long, open jaws of the whale engulfed the book and then all was white: the water, the sky, the land. A blaze of heat and steam electrified the air. Alice was panting when she opened her eyes. There was a glow under the water, soft and luminescent. She watched it fade to a sapphire blue and then turn coal black.

Tex couldn't hold on any longer. He let go and Alice fell, dropping into the water. When she surfaced, he was still floating up above her.

"Sorry, you were too heavy."

"Thanks," she shouted and realized she was only about fifty feet from the bank. The water had receded almost immediately and the boundaries of the lake were clear. The bark of the trees had been stripped by the pounding waves, but the trees were close.

"What about—?" she started in a panicked voice. Tex held up his hands.

"You're sweetie's safe. I found him before I found you. I dragged him over to Old Willie and then came back. Jimmy was out cold. I guess he got smacked in the head by a wave or the whale or something. It was getting so dark I almost didn't find you at all. The whale was the only thing I could see. Where's the book?"

"He ate it." Alice started swimming and Tex bobbed up and down in the air above her until she crawled out of the muddy lake water and collapsed on the embankment. Tex touched down and his knees buckled. He used his hands to support himself as he looked at her.

"Takes a second to get your land legs back."

"I don't think I can move," Alice groaned.

"That was a mighty nice pitch, Alice."

"Thanks."

"I'll fly back to Old Willie. The water's gone down, but they're still on the hill about five or ten miles back. You okay to sit here for awhile?"

"I'm freezing," Alice chattered. Tex pulled his coat off and draped it around her. He turned in a rush and for a second it looked as if he would dive into the cold water of the lake, but then his arms spread out and his body floated on the wind. She saw his silhouette against the rising moon, which shone as silvery and cold as a snowball in the dark.

Chapter Nine

The Return of Miss Goode

(It ain't pretty)

Walter struggled, his feet kicking at the air. He was slammed against the side of the Salvation Army's building with a heavy *thud*. Almost knocked out, he saw stars and bubbles of blue light popping in front of him for a long moment. He shook his vision clear. The hand at his throat, not unlike a steel vise, lowered him until he was eye level. It took Walter a moment to realize whose hand it was, but then he didn't need to go to the outhouse any longer. The front of his pants was now wet. The pale light from the windows slashed out into the side yard and Walter knew everyone was inside among the cheap Halloween decorations, unaware that something far worse than paper skeletons and grinning jack-o-lanterns lurked outside. Count Dracula looked different than he had in the train car. His hair was cut very short and he wore a dark suit. His white shirt was the only spot of color about him. The wind kicked up and the tail of his long overcoat swayed in the breeze. When the vampire smiled under the black fedora, his fangs gleamed in the moonlight. The dark eyes had a soft red sparkle, like rubies in a black, endless sea.

"Hello, Walter. Can you imagine my surprise when I saw you having a nice meal? I came here to recruit men to help transport cargo to Cattersburg. I'll be leaving tonight. You won't have to worry about me again. Now won't that be a relief?"

The Count eased Walter to the ground and dusted off his black jacket. Walter retreated until he hit the wall. The Count chuckled, looming over him. His stark white face was as cold and empty as the moon.

"You don't need to fear me. It's only right to let you live. After all, you released me into this fine new world and I think I owe you something. Your life in exchange for mine? I trust you will let me go." His deep-set eyes glanced upward and he turned his nose to the wind like a wolf catching the smell of prey. Walter heard something, but he thought it was probably just birds flapping somewhere in the night. The Count looked back at him and with rancid breath he leaned close. "Something wicked is in the air. Take care, my friend."

Turning with a snap of his black boots, Dracula strolled into the shadows, his coat billowing behind him. He looked back and Walter could see nothing except his outline and two blood red eyes like garnets catching moonlight under the fedora's brim.

"Incidentally, if you try to track me down...I'll kill your friends, Walter. Centuries ago, I drove thousands of Turkish infidels from my lands. A group of ragged children would be no match for me. I'll drain them dry as dust."

He nodded and then vanished, whistling in the dark.

Walter slumped to the cold grass. His throat hurt from the strength of the vampire's grip. When he touched the sore spots where the sharp nails had dug in, he winced. Looking down and realizing he had wet himself was almost as bad as facing the monster in the darkness. He was too ashamed to go back into the dining hall and it was a long walk back to the train yard where he could get a change of pants. He thought if he waited, maybe the night air would dry them, but he never got to find out. Shouts and screams exploded from the Salvation Army and Walter heard the sound of broken glass. *What now?* he thought, running at full speed around the railing, up the steps and into the dining hall. When he entered the main hall, his mouth fell open and he slid to a complete stop. The last remains of a collective gasp echoed through the crowded room.

Effigy Goode stood at the double doors at the front of the hall wearing a smug smile. She was also wearing her pink nightgown from the night before, but it was soiled on the front. Her pink slippers had turned brown from mud. Walter knew something bad was happening because Bob had John sheltered behind him in a protective way. Everyone was so silent that he could hear the soft bubbling of boiling soup from the kitchen. Walter walked down the long row of tables, his shoes making a *clunking* sound against the wood floor, and approached Bob from behind. Miss Goode snarled.

"There's another one. Where are the others? I don't want

them to miss this." She reached up and touched the golden cap sitting on her head. It was a shiny material, reflecting the light with encrusted jewels around the band.

"Effigy," Bob began in a soothing voice. The dining hall was dead quiet as he spoke. "I know this has been a difficult few days, but there's nothing that can't be made right."

"My store is smashed!"

"You can fix that," Bob announced. "It's just glass and wood and brick, but I won't allow you to hurt these children."

"I hate to contradict you, Robert," she belted out, her shrill laughter echoing, "but pain is inevitable when scolding naughty children! I want these little darlings to get exactly what they deserve and you can't make an omelet without breaking a few eggs."

"It's not that simple. These children are trying to get everything back the way it was before the books were opened. They are risking their lives every moment to save this town. To save the world."

"How noble."

"Listen, we've taken care of the Revolutionary War."

"We did that all by ourselves," John shouted from behind Bob's arm.

"The others are attempting to get the dinosaurs and Moby Dick back home where they belong, but we've got lots more to do. Count Dracula is still loose and if we don't stop him, do you know what could happen?"

"A regrettable loss," she shrugged.

"Regrettable loss?" Bob repeated with wide eyes. "Is that all you can say? That monster will go on feeding forever if we don't find and destroy him."

"You won't be able to get them all back in, so there's no need to try. Just accept what you can do and move on," she jeered.

"You're a very smart woman," Bob said. "You would never run a business like this."

"I suppose letting Santa Claus whisk you all away at my expense was funny, eh? You like opening those books and using them to your own advantage, do you?"

"Well..." Bob began, but she cut him off, her voice reverberating around the room.

"Well, I know how to use the books too, Robert! Have you forgotten?"

"No, I haven't."

"I thought I'd bring one down and let you and these precious little gems take a trip. Would you like that, children? Your sweet Miss Goode is going to send you on a long journey."

"Stay back," Bob warned her. Miss Goode only giggled.

"They won't grow up, they won't grow old and they'll never die. What could be better than that? I'm thinking this book will suit you."

Miss Goode held out a dusty leather copy in front of her. Bob read the title on the cover and he began backing up with Walter and John tucked behind him. Miss Goode chuckled.

"What's wrong, Bob? Dante's *Inferno* not the best way to spend eternity? You and those meddling little warts can enjoy all nine circles of hell! Come here and take your medicine like good little boys."

"Now you can't d-do that, Effigy," Bob stammered. "The only way real, living beings can go into the books is if something from inside is being forced back in."

"Just what I had in mind," she cooed. "I thought I would open a few pages. A thousand demons can tear this little town apart within the hour and when I send them back to hell, you and those little scallywags can go with them!"

"Hey, lady?" One of the hobos stood up. "I don't know what's going on here, but we ain't gonna let you hurt no little kids."

"That's right," another voice echoed. Effigy Goode threw back her head and laughed so hard tears slid down her cheeks. Her face went bright red from the laughter and Bob realized she had gone completely insane.

Her hair was wild and caked with grass.

Her one good eye peered from her skull as beady and black as a shark.

Her hands were drenched in dirt to her elbows.

"What do you think of my new hat?" she asked through the hysterical laughing fit.

"It doesn't do much for you," John said, peeking around Bob's waist. Miss Goode looked at him with a face of steely resolution and then took a long, labored breath into her body. Her laughter was gone. Something horrid and violent flashed in her one eye and, if possible, it seemed to get blacker.

"There's my little monkey now. I pulled this lovely hat from a safe place at home. It's a special hat, little monkey. Let me show you just what I can do with it!"

Miss Goode threw her arms up and shouted. The doors

behind her splintered from the frame and crashed inward under the weight. A swirling dark mass of wings and furry arms flew into the dining hall. People began to scream. Men and women toppled over each other trying to get to the back of the dining hall. Some hobos crawled under the long tables while others escaped out the back door. Miss Goode continued shouting and laughing, waving her arms as the ceiling swirled with dark, quivering shadows. Bob, John and Walter stared in shock at the flying monkeys that soared into the rafters of the room. The dark, small bodies were held aloft by the wings jutting from their backs, and they were all different. A variety of primates swung from the light fixtures and soared through the air: chimps, rhesus monkeys, and lemurs. The wings were different too. Some had brown, leathery wings like bats. Other had feathers with all manner of colors. Chattering filled the air as they swooped down, picking at the food on the tables.

A scream from the kitchen caused everyone to turn. Volunteers came flooding into the main hall, food in their hair and monkeys flying after them, hammering on pots and pans with large ladles. The monkeys continued hopping around, stealing bits of food or sitting perched on the window ledges like sentinels. An oversized flying monkey swiped a necklace from a woman's throat. She screamed and promptly fainted. Miss Goode brought her hands down and shouted, "Enough!"

The chattering of the monkeys died off. Sobs of fear echoed from under tables, in closets, and around the perimeter of the room. Miss Goode was wearing an awful smile. Bob turned to John and grabbed him by the shoulders. "I'm sorry I didn't tell you before, but I was going to...I promise. She's not your aunt."

"*What?*"

"Your aunt's been missing for years."

"Who is she?" John muttered, looking around Bob's side at the nightmarish woman in a tattered pink nightgown. Bob gulped.

"She's the Wicked Witch of the West."

"I'm not sure I can take much more of this," Walter mumbled, slapping a hand to his head. John stared at Bob with wide eyes and his small fingers dug into Bob's trousers, his grip tightening in fear.

"That's right," Miss Goode sighed. "I ruled the Winkies for years, even drove the Great Oz from my lands with the help of these monkeys and who are you to trifle with me? Your aunt found the books and opened them. I wasn't what she was expecting, but here I am and here I'll stay."

"Her powers are limited," Bob shouted shielding Walter and John. "She's been here too long and her magic isn't what it used to be."

"True," Miss Goode acknowledged with a faint nod. "Robert is quite accurate, children, but this cap is something I've been saving for many years. It allows me to summon the monkeys from the book to do my bidding. This is all the power I'll ever need. My minions heed my commands."

Miss Goode glared upward into the rafters full of swinging monkeys. "You!" she snapped. A large monkey with a misshapen head came soaring from the window ledge. He swooped down and landed at her side. He snorted and turned his head as the witch reached down and touched the black fur covering his crown.

"Those three I want taken alive," she growled, pointing at Walter, Bob and John. "Take them to my home and tie them up in the cellar until we can find the others. Have your army kill the rest of these miserable wretches. Rip out their eyes and tear the limbs from their bodies."

"As you command," the monkey grumbled. Walter, Bob and John were all shocked to hear the winged creature speak. After all they had witnessed over the last few days, it shouldn't have surprised them, but it did. The leader of the flying monkeys signaled to the others and people started to scream as they leaped into the air. Bob held Walter and John close, his arms wrapped around their heads for protection as the fierce monkeys swarmed their way. A man in a gray wool suit went screaming toward the back wall with three monkeys flapping at his head, their fingers hooked into his hair and collar. A woman in a sack dress came *whooping* by, her feet inches above the ground as two monkeys lifted her into the air and tried to pull her in different directions. A young man tried to run and was hoisted by a monkey through a window. Plates, glasses and silverware all went flying around the room or crashed to the floor.

"STOP!!!" a voice yelled and the monkeys paused, the beating of their wings making the room hum. Miss Goode looked around, startled. Walter lowered Bob's arm from his eyes and searched the mess to find who had called out. A gust of wind whipped through the broken doorway and Jimmy, Alice and Tex flew in, sprinkled with Tinkerbell's magic dust. Miss Goode ducked as they soared into the room, but Jimmy was too fast. His hand snagged the cap from her head and he arched upward toward the ceiling. Miss Goode let out a shriek. Pointing a long finger at him, she began to stamp her feet and scream.

"THAT'S MINE!! KILL HIM! BRING ME THAT CAP!"

The winged monkeys all stared in wonder, without moving. Effigy Goode snarled.

"DIDN'T YOU HEAR ME? WHAT'S WRONG WITH YOU INFERNAL CREATURES? BRING ME THAT CAP? YOU HAVE TO DO AS I COMMAND!"

"No," the monkey leader grunted. "We have to obey the one who wears the cap."

Jimmy slapped the cap on his head as Alice soared down and landed by Bob. John ran to her, wrapping his arms around her neck. Tex touched down next to Walter with one eyebrow arched.

"Fancy flying, huh?"

"Show off." Walter chuckled.

"Listen to me," Jimmy announced with his voice echoing through the hall. "I am a powerful sorcerer. I have the cap and I am in command now."

"He's a phony! A fake!" Miss Goode laughed. "Can't you see that?"

"He can *fly*," the monkey leader hissed and Miss Goode screamed.

"HE'S JUST A ROUSTABOUT! GIVE ME THE CAP!"

"Get her," Jimmy said calmly and the monkeys slid their dark eyes toward Miss Goode. She gasped, turned and ran into the darkness, screaming. Her pink silk nightgown fluttered in the wind as she bolted down the sidewalk. Dozens of monkeys swooped through the broken doorway after her.

Jimmy snapped his fingers and the head monkey flew up to greet him with a bow.

"We are at your service."

"Take her back to her house and tie her up. Guard the house so that no one gets in or out until we arrive. Is that understood?"

"Yes, mighty sorcerer." The wings flapped twice and the monkey pivoted in midair, sailing out the doors into the night. Jimmy lowered himself to the floor. People were coming out from under the tables to face the mess. A low rumble of voices started to drift through the room.

"Well, well, well...mighty sorcerer, huh?" Tex chuckled. "You're a little young to be that mighty, aren't you?"

"Who ever heard of a thirteen-year-old sorcerer?" Jimmy scoffed, pulling the cap from his head and stuffing it in his back pocket.

"Guess the flying monkeys have."

John ran over and scooped up the copy of Dante's *Inferno* from the floor and handed it to Bob, who made sure the buckle was secure and then tucked it under his arm.

"How did it go?" John asked. Alice smiled.

"Newton stopped the dinosaurs."

"All right!" John cheered.

"I was almost a snack." Tex nodded fiercely. "A flying one was this close to having a Tex Sandwich."

"You saw a Pterodactyl?" Walter asked with his mouth agape.

"The whale's gone too." Alice sighed.

Tex grinned. "Makes me feel like fish for supper."

"Let's get you something hot to eat," Bob was saying, but

Jimmy and Alice, still damp from the water, waved him off.

"There's no time. Let's get to Miss Goode's place. We'll see if we can't find the rest of the books. She'll have to tell us where they are eventually."

"She'll never talk," John said, turning to his sister with a quizzical look on his face. "Did you have any idea she was a *real* witch?"

Alice shook her head and shrugged.

"We've got bigger problems," Walter announced. They all stood silent while he told them the story of running into the Count outside. Jimmy listened with his eyes trained on the floor and then set his mouth into a tight slit.

"Okay. Miss Goode's not going anywhere. The monkeys will see to that. We'll crack that nut later. If Dracula is trying to leave from Cattersburg, boy...that station is at least twenty miles from here. Tex?" Jimmy asked, turning and staring at the boy's red hair and freckled face. "Cattersburg? What train would he be taking?"

"Huh? Oh. Well, let me see...Cattersburg." Tex began running through the train schedules and stops in his head. His eyes floated to the top of his head and he scratched his chin. "Got to be the 9:05 L&N. No fastballs going out of there on a Thursday night, only slow freighters. He might be southbound toward Atlanta if he's looking to pick up a passenger car. Otherwise, he'd have to go northeast on the freight service lines headed toward Knoxville, or maybe some of the smaller towns along the way. The line ends in Cincinnati."

Bob cleared his throat. "Dracula told Walter he hired men to help move cargo. In the book, he goes to England with large wooden crates. They were filled with the soil from his burial place. They acted as a sort of mobile grave for him. That's what you're looking for—large crates of Romanian soil. He's been busy. He's gone into the book and pulled out untold numbers of crates. That way he'll have places to rest in the daylight hours, and he could scatter them all over the country or even the world if he wanted."

"How many of these things did he have in the book?"

"Around fifty, I think."

Jimmy pulled the golden cap from his pocket and stuffed it on John's head. "There you go, Big John. You've got all the power over the flying monkeys. They'll do exactly as you command."

"Looks like Buck Rogers." Tex snickered.

John put his hands firmly on his hips and his face shifted toward the rafters with pride. "I'm Jack Armstrong, All American Boy!" he shouted in homage to one of his favorite radio programs. Jimmy stifled his smile, winked at Alice and clamped a hand on John's shoulder.

"You and Bob head over to Goode's house and wait for us, John. We'll make it to Cattersburg and search the cars. We'll find the Count and destroy him."

"We don't have weapons," Walter pleaded.

"We'll have to make do," Alice shrugged. "We can break down the harpoons and they'll act as wooden stakes. You said that's how they got him in the picture."

"I'll see if they have a crucifix or cross around here," Bob offered, and then added. "And the kitchen may have some garlic. Wait right here, I'll be back."

"I still have this one," Walter said, pulling the tarnished crucifix from his coat pocket and running his fingers over the metal surface.

"Can we fly?" Jimmy asked and Alice shook her head. She reached out beside her and flapped her arms.

"It's gone. The extra burst of dust we got when we met up with Old Willie and the boys was just enough to get us here. We could go back to the hobo jungle."

"No time," Jimmy said. Pitching his voice over the noise of the main hall, he got everyone's attention. "Excuse me! We need a lift to Cattersburg tonight, right now! Can someone help us please? Please? It's a matter of life and death!"

"I'll help you, son," a grizzled old man said, stepping forward. "Can't thank you enough for saving us. We were just about done for after those flying critters got in here. My truck is out back. I'll take you anywhere you want to go."

"Thank you," Jimmy sighed with relief. He gave Tex and Alice and Walter an encouraging smile.

Chapter Ten

Facing the Undead

The Cattersburg station was smaller than the Carson Corners train yard. Jimmy, Alice, Tex and Walter hopped from the back of the truck, waved good-bye to the old guy who had brought them, and hid in the shadows near the depot. The high waters blocking trains going in and out of Carson Corners had forced many hobos to catch out in Cattersburg. Many of them were ambling about, waiting to hop on board. Stout bulls prowled the L&N Railway. The locomotive was as black as the darkness around them. Jimmy scouted out the fields and trees beyond the station and knew dozens of men and woman were waiting to hop on when the train got going.

"How can we search the cars with so much activity?" Alice whispered.

Jimmy thought about it for a moment, staring at the cattle cars in front of them. Jimmy and Tex had made stakes from their harpoons on the ride through the dark wintry landscape, breaking them down into two-foot shafts. He stuffed his stake into the belt of his overalls and set his face into a grim determination.

"We gotta split up."

"I'm scared," Walter said and everyone looked at him. Alice put her hand on his arm.

"So am I," she agreed.

"No," Walter grumbled, shaking his head. "You don't understand. I'm the only one who has seen him. I've come face-to-face with him twice and I'm telling you, he's *very* dangerous."

"Well, excuse me," Tex said. "Gettin' through the Revolutionary War wasn't a walk in the park."

"Actually it was," Alice mused. "Remember, we ended up in the park?"

Tex became more annoyed. "You know what I mean! It wasn't easy. Trying to get that whale back in the book about did us all in, Walt. We barely got out of that alive."

"We don't have the book with us," Walter explained. His voice was quivering. "Don't you see? There's no flash of light, no trapping him back in the pages where he belongs. *He's* got the book."

Jimmy nodded and then slapped his hand on Walter's shoulder. "It means we'll have to destroy him. You're not having doubts, are you?"

"No, of course not. I just think that the longer the characters are out, the more they start to evolve. I think if the author didn't describe something well enough, the characters fill in the gaps. He might be more powerful than he was even in the book. The Count could be faster, smarter, have different motivations. What I'm getting at is...well, destroying a real vampire isn't something you do at the drop of a hat."

"We don't have a choice," Jimmy said. "We let him out, we have to finish it. Now Alice's brother is waiting on us back at Miss Goode's house. Bob wants to go back to his family in *A Christmas Carol*. The other people who have been stuck in this world working for Miss Goode want to go home. We need to make sure no one ever gets near those books again. All that stuff we've still got to make right, but for now…let's 23 skidoo."

Walter nodded and took out his crucifix, rubbing the tarnished metal in his fingers. Bob had found enough garlic that he and Alice had strung the bulbs together and made a necklace. Alice slipped it over her head and dropped it around Walter's neck in the shadows. "No, Alice, you need it. Bob said the garlic would help protect us against him."

"I can't stand the smell," she whispered and smiled with a wink.

"We'll all be headed in pretty much the same direction, but it'll look less suspicious if we're scattered than all together. If anyone finds anything, give a whistle," Jimmy said and they were off, scattering around the depot. Walter scurried around a group of abandoned orange crates and ran south behind the depot. He ran through high weeds, his legs pumping as he cleared the depot, peering around the platform. Two yard bulls strolled along with clubs in their beefy hands. Walter waited till they passed and then bolted from his spot in the shadows. He ran through the gravel along the tracks, peeking in at the cars. Footsteps crunching through the gravel nearby made him turn and see Tex not more than fifty feet behind him, rechecking the cars. Walter glanced up at a *click-click-click* sound above him. Jimmy was running along the top of a reefer car. It made Walter feel better, safer to know his friends were all around him. Walter ran farther down the tracks until he neared the end of the line.

"Pssssttt," someone hissed and Walter saw Tex's dark shape motioning him back. Tex slid the door of a one-eyed jack and pointed inside. Walter could see the large crates stacked against the far corner of the car. At one time the car, with wooden beams throughout for support, looked to have been a mail baggage car. Peeling white paint crumbled from the wooden walls. Walter put two fingers in his mouth and gave a quick whistle. Jimmy and Alice were there beside them in what seemed like seconds, looking inside the car as well.

"It smells funny," Jimmy said, pulling a handkerchief from his pocket and tying it around his face. He stuffed the corner in his shirt collar so it covered his nose and mouth completely.

"Yeah," Alice agreed, pinching her nose.

"It's just the garlic," Tex snorted, waving his hand in front of his face and taking two steps away from Walter. "Whew, that stuff is powerful."

"It makes me feel...." Alice began, but couldn't find the words to finish.

"Like you're getting sick," Walter finished for her. "It's the dirt inside the crates. It's the smell of death."

"More bums!" a voice shouted and they all turned with a start. Walter shoved the crucifix out in front of him for protection. The two yard bulls had circled back and were standing a few feet away, swinging their clubs. The lights of the depot were behind the bulls, so no one in the group could see their faces, only two bulky, dark outlines. One wore a cap and the other a cowboy hat. A voice came chuckling from the darkness.

"You planning on robbing the train, son?" a thick voice called, and it was more than obvious the guy had been hitting the bottle. His words were slurred. Jimmy realized everyone was looking at him. He pulled his handkerchief down and shrugged.

"What about you? Gonna preach at us?"

Walter lowered his cross. He spoke up with his voice set in determination.

"Look here, gentlemen, you've got a vampire trying to ship boxes of burial soil on this train."

A long pause followed Walter's words and then an explosion of laughter rocked the silence. The two silhouettes stumbled back, staggering near the tracks as they held onto each other for support and laughed until they cried.

"Nice going," Tex muttered into Walter's ear. "They think we're looney-tooney."

Jimmy laughed as well. Alice, Walter and Tex all looked at him, shocked. "He's not talking about *real* vampires," Jimmy chuckled. "He means *Vampires of the Road.*"

The laughter ceased. The yard bulls inched closer, wiping tears from their faces. They turned and Walter could see more of their faces than before: strong, brutish, high foreheads, thick necks. One of them spit a stream of tobacco into the weeds. "Gangs huh?" he mumbled and Jimmy nodded.

"Yes, sir."

"Well, they'll jack roll you bums blind, but as far as we're concerned a bum is a bum. Makes no difference how you size it up. You're all freeloaders. The gangs are your problem, not ours."

"Yes sir," Jimmy agreed.

"What are *Vampires of the Road?*" Alice whispered to Walter. He leaned over and whispered back in her ear.

"They are wandering gangs who rob from other hobos. They always wear black shirts and hats."

"Now," the shorter of the two bulls announced, "we got to run you all in. Sheriff's been looking for some workers for the new highway. I think y'all will do just dandy."

"We can't do that," Tex said after a short pause. He hitched up his overalls and stepped forward, dropping his hands on his hips. "I'm sorry boys, but we're on a mission here. It's a *green light.*"

"What did you say?"

"You heard me," Tex snapped. "Now you can get on out of here and bother some other 'bo's, but we gotta catch this-here train."

"You're a dead kid," the shorter one said, slapping his club against his open palm.

"Can't catch us all," Tex said and, like lightening, they scattered. Walter grabbed hold of Alice's hand and they took off to the left, Jimmy to the right and Tex scampered up over the car connection and landed on the other side of the freight car in a dead run. The bulls started shouting and running after them, but were confused at first. A whistle's shrill call hit the wind and other bulls came running from the depot.

Alice and Walter hid in the trees.

"My heart feels like it's going to break outta my chest," she gasped. Walter put his hands on his knees and leaned over, trying to get some air. When he stood up, he gave her a weary smile.

"I grabbed your hand because you didn't know the password. When Tex said *green light*, that was our signal to make a bolt for it."

"You think Jimmy and Tex are okay?"

"Sure, they're always okay. I've never seen two boys get in more scrapes than those two and they always come out smiling. If the train starts to pull out from here, those bulls will be waiting to knock us in the head. Let's take cover behind the tree line and see if we can get farther down the tracks."

Walter and Alice circled through the dark woods, keeping a wary eye on the depot a few hundred feet away. When they had circled all the way around in front of the train, they left the safety of the trees and walked the tracks down the line. Walter eased them into some high grass and waited.

"The train's just starting to roll. Now, Alice, this is a double header and it's gonna move fast. We have to be ready, all right?"

"I'll keep up."

"If you don't think you can get on, then don't try. Make your way back to Carson Corners and wait for us."

She nodded. The sleek cars moved down the track toward them. Walter waited until enough of the train had passed them, wheels rolling on the tracks, and then he pulled her with him. They ran alongside the tracks and

Walter counted the cars until he saw the one with the Count's crates. He made a leap, took the metal rung of the ladder in his hand and swung inside gracefully. He turned and stretched out his hand. Alice ran as fast as she could, her boots slapping against the gravel. Their fingers touched for a brief moment. Walter reached farther out. Jimmy and Tex came rushing from the back of the car, holding Walter's coat from behind as he leaned way out and snagged Alice's hand in his own. He hoisted her into the train car and she collided into Jimmy, both of them falling on the floor and rolling toward the crates.

"You okay?" Jimmy asked helping Alice up.

"I'm fine," Alice said. "Thanks, Walter, you really saved my life."

"Don't mention it," he shrugged. Tex stood back and whistled.

"Would you look at all those boxes?"

Alice pulled some candle stubs from her pockets as Tex did likewise. They lit them all and the train car turned warm in the glow.

"C'mon," Jimmy said, and they spread out. Tex opened the first crate, peering down inside where a swarm of rats rolled and writhed. He slammed the lid with a scream. Everyone turned and looked at him, startled.

"What is it?" Jimmy hissed. "Is it him? Is he in there?"

"Nobody said anything about *rats*! I hate 'em!!"

Jimmy chuckled and Alice smiled. They all went back to searching, ripping open crate after crate. The creaking of wood and the sounds of their breathing were masked by the wind rattling through the half-open door. Jimmy and Tex lifted a crate out of the way and started going through the one beneath it. Alice and Walter shoved aside several crates that they had gone through and used them as steps to some of the higher ones. Their shadows were large and monstrous on the walls. Walter hammered at the lid of one crate and threw it open to find only dirt and mold and rat droppings. Alice peeled the lid back from another and two rats sat inside with dark eyes staring at her. She shut the lid with a groan.

"I'm with Tex...no more rats."

The train had the earth trembling for a mile on each side. The world rushed by at incredible speeds and the wind whipped through the door, making the candle flames flicker and dance.

Walter slid another lid open and found only wet soil and a smell like the town dump back in Boise. He started to close the lid and then noticed something odd sticking out of the dirt. A corner of something was protruding from the black soil. Walter placed his candle down inside the makeshift coffin and brushed the dirt away. The leather-bound cover of the book came into view. Walter lifted it from the sticky earth and hopped down to the floor.

"You found the book," Alice squealed with delight. Tex and Jimmy all leaped over the crates and dropped to the floor. Walter set the book on the lid of a crate.

"Let's get on with it," Tex shouted.

"There's nothing to do," Jimmy huffed.

"I guess we wait?" Walter asked.

"Yep," Jimmy sighed. "When the Count comes to take possession of these crates, he'll find us here to stop him."

Walter looked up with a strange frown crossing his face.

Jimmy noticed it right away and put a hand on the boy's shoulder. "What is it, Walter?"

"Why would he leave the book? It seems so…odd to leave it unguarded."

"I didn't," a voice hissed. They all jerked into action, fanning out around the car. Walter picked the book up and clutched it to his chest against the wreath of garlic. He held the crucifix out, swinging his arm left and right, but the train car was empty. The strange flickering candlelight created twisting shadows on the walls as they pivoted in small circles, trying to find the voice. A scattering of noise slithered overhead.

"He's on the roof," Jimmy whispered.

"I'll get 'im," Tex shouted and started for the train car door, but Alice pulled him back. The scuttling sound slid over the side of the car and the Count's pale face peered at them, upside down, from the door. All of them jumped back. His hand, bone white, curled around the train door and threw it open so hard it slammed against the wall, cracking and splintering on impact. The twisted sound of metal screamed as the door bounced back and jammed on its track. The Count crawled in across the ceiling beams like a roach and snarled. He leaped to the floor with his black overcoat billowing in the wind. His sharp teeth were made even more frightening in the candlelight.

"Welcome," he hissed in a voice less than human. "Secretly, I was hoping you would come, Walter. By dawn, we'll all be far away from here. I think this one will suit you just fine." The Count extended one long claw and pointed to a crate.

162

"You ain't so scary," Tex shouted, pulling one of the stakes from his belt.

"Let's get him," Jimmy shouted, arching the stake over his head as Tex did likewise. Walter held the crucifix out and the same white light he'd seen before brightened the train car. The vampire hissed, drawing back from the light of the crucifix, his blood red eyes glowing. Walter advanced with the book. He unbuckled the leather strap and was opening the pages when it happened. The Count snagged Tex's collar and drew back, sending Tex flying through the door out into the darkness. For a long, horrifying moment Alice, Jimmy and Walter stood in shock, unmoving. They stared into the rushing wind and darkness, the countryside peppered with tiny lights, until the horror hit them full-force.

"TEX!!" Alice screamed. She ran toward the open door with some fleeting thought he was hanging outside, waiting for them to rescue him. She kept replaying it in her mind, thinking, *He's holding onto the ladder, he's holding onto the ladder.* The Count was fast as lightening. He curled his fingers in her hair and snapped her back against him. Alice screamed and fought, her hands slapping at the iron claw holding her in place. Jimmy charged, trying to save Alice and the Count knocked the stake from his hand. In a flash the vampire had Jimmy by the back of the neck. He held them roughly and gave them a shake, snarling. There were no whites to his eyes, only a deep burgundy color like dried blood. The black pupils slid inside that red sea and grew wider, staring Walter down.

"First, throw away that abomination or I'll kill another one," Count Dracula snapped with his fangs clenched in fury. Alice screamed as he tightened his grip. Walter drew back and threw the crucifix out into the rushing wind and the dazzling white glow went with it. The eerie candlelight returned and the Count smiled. "That's my good boy."

"Please let them go," Walter managed to say. He was trying not to think about Tex, but the tears were starting to bubble in his eyes. The image of Tex's broken body out in the night was causing him to quiver all over. "P-please!"

"Second...give me the book."

"No, Walter," Jimmy grunted through gritted teeth.

"No," Alice managed to utter. "Don't give it to him!"

"I'll break her neck," the Count sang. "Would you like that, Walter?"

Jimmy grunted. "Send us with him back into the book!"

"Don't listen to them," Dracula growled. "They think the world would be better off without me, but I'm not so bad. I want to survive just like anyone else. Wouldn't you do anything to save your friends, Walter? Give me the book and I'll give you their lives in exchange. If not, they'll sleep like the dead."

"Okay." Walter held it out with shaky fingers.

"Throw it over there," the Count commanded and Walter tossed it into the shadows. It hit the floor behind three of the large crates, sliding in the dirt. The Count dragged Jimmy and Alice with him. He circled around and blocked Walter from the back of the train car. Now the Count was positioned between Walter and the book.

"Let them go," Walter said. The vampire closed his eyes and shook his head in a steady, creepy rhythm. His lips curled back and his fangs were highlighted in shadow.

"As I said, I think this crate will do fine. You will be nice and warm down in the dirt. As for the thirst...well, we'll ride the night trains together. So many poor souls scattered along the rails. No one will miss them. Just let me kill these two and then you and I will sit down and have a nice, long talk in the dark."

Bob Cratchit sat in Miss Goode's parlor having a cup of tea. Winged monkeys hopped and flew through the house, tearing at the curtains, going through the kitchen drawers and generally making a mess. Their chittering noises were almost overwhelming. He looked up and found three of them swinging on the chandelier. Miss Goode was upstairs in her bedroom of velvet and silk, strapped down in a huge Louis XVI chair with a scarf stuffed in her mouth. John was having a great time. Wearing the golden cap, he had proclaimed himself King of the Winged Monkeys and had organized a sing-along upstairs while they danced around Miss Goode and chanted. At first, she had been frightened and wailed into the scarf, but now it had grown tiresome. She sat there with a burning expression in her one good eye and her teeth clamped together over the scarf in pure, white-hot rage.

Bob took his tea and walked outside on to the front porch where more winged monkeys swung from the eaves. They hopped along the roof of the three-level, yellow and white house, flew around the chimneys, chased each other through the open windows of the second floor and made a chain hanging from each other's tails down the rose trellis. Some of them sat on the widow's walk, scanning the skies. Bob walked out on the lawn, stepped in monkey poop, and then walked to the end of the lane with a sigh.

The sky was beginning to brighten in the east. The first gray glow of daylight backed the leafless trees in the distance. A fight had broken out behind him on the roof, but Bob didn't bother turning around. One monkey had something the others wanted, *yet again*, and the squawking, shrieking and chattering was at full volume. He took a sip of tea and wondered where Alice, Jimmy, Tex and Walter could be. They had been gone all night. John was having too much fun to notice how late it was, but Bob was feeling nervous. All the books were stashed in a safe place in the train yard. He felt good about that point. Miss Goode was out of commission for a while and he felt *very* good about point number two. Third, almost all the creatures and people known to have escaped from the pages had been returned to the books no worse for wear.

The uneven field beyond the house sloped down to the main road. Bob could see someone walking, or rather stumbling, through the shadowy trees at the end of the lane. He watched for a long time as the cold light of morning continued to break. The shadow moved up the road, hobbling. As the figure grew closer, Bob thought there was something familiar about the shabby clothing. As the light shifted over the trees, he caught a glint of reflection off the boy's glasses. He dropped his teacup in the grass and started running. His heart was hammering, but he didn't care. He cleared the fields and hit the dirt road with a stitch in his side.

"Walter!" he shouted, clutching a hand to his side. The

boy looked up with a dirt-stained face and burst into tears. Bob could tell his leg was hurt, but the boy began to hobble even faster, kicking up dirt. Bob rushed up just in time to catch Walter in his arms as he fell forward. Bob collapsed into the dust with Walter's head cradled in his lap.

"What happened?" he whispered, removing Walter's filthy glasses. The boy stared up into the first light of morning.

"Help me," he whispered through the sobs. "The books...I need them."

Chapter Eleven

Setting the Clocks: Spring Forward, Fall Back

The monkeys were silent. They perched on the newel post, stood in doorways and hopped outside the windows, their wings barely flapping as Walter lay stretched on the parlor loveseat, unconscious. John stood nearby with a bowl of water and a washcloth. Bob tried to clean the dirt and soot from Walter's tear-stained face. Bob looked over and was proud of John. The boy stood still, his golden cap titled to one side and his face calm as he watched Walter with concern. Bob dipped the washcloth into the water. He placed it over Walter's forehead. The boy's bright eyes flew open in alarm. He slapped his face in a frantic fight to find his glasses. Bob placed his hands on Walter's shoulders and took the glasses, still covered with dirt and grit, from a small end table and put them back on his head. Walter glanced around the room, breathing in great heaves.

"It's all right," Bob said. "You're safe."

"Is A-Alice okay?" John stammered. Bob turned to him and spoke firmly.

"He's had a rough night, John. I want you to go out and close the door. See if you can get Miss Goode to tell you where she keeps her liquor. If not, search around the kitchen and see if you can find some whiskey or port. Walter's had a bad shock."

Bob hustled John and all the monkeys out, then closed the drawing room doors. He waited, pausing at the oak doors for a long moment. It was several minutes, but he heard John's footsteps moving toward the kitchen. A series of thumps followed and Bob knew the monkeys were leaping down from their places to follow him. Bob walked back to the velvet sofa and slipped another lace pillow under Walter's head. The boy was looking up with an empty expression. Waiting a beat, Bob nodded and then held Walter's hand.

"Tell me what happened."

"The books we hid in the train yard—"

"They're right here," Bob said, patting the metal chest sitting by an eighteenth-century rosewood clock. "You collapsed outside asking about them. I was afraid someone, or *something*, had gotten to them. John ordered some of the monkeys to fly into town and retrieve them, but they're fine. They are all there. I checked."

"Give them to me." Bob slid them over. He threw open the chest.

"See, they're all fine. I counted them myself."

"Bring them closer," Walter said. Bob dragged the chest beside the loveseat and Walter's dirty fingers began scrambling through them. His eyes were wild.

"Walter, what happened?" Bob urged

"It was awful," he started, his hands still rifling through the books. "We found the crates on a freight train out of Cattersburg. We caught it as it was leaving the station, about four hundred feet away from the depot. I found the book down inside one of the crates, but he was there."

"Dracula?"

"He threw Tex out the doorway."

Bob stifled a shocked cry. Walter looked at him and then went on.

"He made me throw the book into the back of the train car. He had Jimmy and Alice by the throat and said he'd kill them if I didn't. I just wanted him to leave them alone so I did."

"What happened?" Bob urged, his face growing pale.

"He broke Alice's neck and bit Jimmy in the throat. I just stood there, watching, while Jimmy screamed and bled all over the train car."

"How did you get here?"

"I jumped."

"What?" Bob asked in disbelief.

"I knew I'd probably die anyway so it didn't matter. I was going to be killed by the Count or I could take my chances jumping. I've hopped off freighters before going fast, but this was a double header. We had slowed for some reason. I don't know why, but I knew it was the only chance I'd get, so I threw myself out into the fields. I think I was knocked out because when I woke up there were cows around and the moon was higher in the sky. I started back, but I must have twisted my ankle in the fall."

"You poor boy," Bob said, his lips quivering.

"On my way back, I looked for Tex, but I never found him. I don't know what happened, but his body has got to be out there...somewhere."

"It's all right, Walter." Bob pulled Walter up and crushed him to his chest in a hug, then he took in a long, hard breath.

"I don't want you to worry about a thing. We'll get these monkeys and Miss Goode a one-way ticket back to Oz, and if she won't tell us where *The Wonderful Wizard of Oz* is, we'll send them into one of the books we have available. Tinkerbell can fly back to Never Never Land because we do have the copy of *Peter Pan*. We'll stash those books where no one will find them. We'll leave town...you and me and John."

"You don't care about getting home?"

"Not any longer. I've been living here for all these years, missing a home that I never really had anyway. It was all just part of a story...pen on paper. I guess I am home. I think it's better to be real than fiction, don't you? You and John and I will start a new life somewhere."

Walter coughed and Bob's eyes went wide. He reached down and rubbed a finger against Walter's lips. It came away red.

"You're bleeding."

"I think I hit pretty hard." Walter nodded. "There's something wrong inside me. I had to walk back in the cold and I don't know how far down the track we'd gotten when I jumped. I've been coughing up blood all night. It seems like I remember somebody giving me a ride in the back of a cattle truck somewhere along the way. I don't know. I can't remember."

"We'll fetch a doctor."

"No, not now. Bob, are you sure that if something happens to the books, it just closes the door to getting back where you belong?"

"I don't know...that's what I assumed would happened. Why?"

"The Count was obsessed with getting the book back even though he had all those crates of earth. He didn't need that book any longer, but he killed Jimmy and Alice for it. I think we've underestimated the books. It's a lifeline. I can make it right again."

"What do you mean?"

Walter began digging through the chest of books again and Bob watched him with steady eyes. He reached out and clamped his hand on Walter's wrist. The boy's skin was icy cold.

"I don't know what you're thinking, but you're not a character in these books, Walter. There's no life written for you there, so you'd see everything like watching the world through a windowpane. You'll only exist between the *words*."

"I don't want to get in," he whispered.

"There's nothing you can let out of those books that will make it right."

"Yes, there is...*time*."

Walter pushed Bob's hand away and kept sorting through the musty leather copies. He let out a long, low, rattling sigh when he found the one he wanted. Walter collapsed back on the loveseat and stared with wide, wondering eyes at the cover. He turned the book around and held up the title for Bob to see. Walter's trembling fingers pulled the strap through the buckle.

"Are you sure about this?" Bob asked.

"I thought about it all night walking back here. I remembered it from the first time we found the books. It was down toward the bottom. I didn't give it much of a thought then, but I have to do it. I have to *save* them."

"Please be careful. All of you come back safely," Bob said and, with a nod, he left the room, closing the double doors behind him. Walter lay on the loveseat. He felt cold on the outside, hot on the inside. He coughed again and could taste the blood. Muted voices from beyond the doors echoed in the house. Walter looked at the book resting on his lap: *Theories of Time Travel.* He looked up and prayed.

"Please, God, please let this work."

Walter threw open the book and a blaze of light came rushing out. He felt heat prickling all over his body and he could see a wall of hazy clouds fill the room. He saw black writing, like a quill pen would produce, begin to fill up the room, hundreds of thousands of lines of pages soaring upward into the sky. The house was gone. The town was gone. Nothing but light and wind and a tunnel of mist like the eye of a hurricane. Walter saw events from the last hours in front of him projected onto the clouds like a movie reel. He could see everything happening in reverse. Out of the dark and wind, there was the Count moving so swiftly that Walter thought he was imagining it. Tex came flying back into the train car as it continued reversing. Time was speeding up. It all started going faster: finding the book, crates, pulling Alice up into the car, running along the tracks. Walter tried to close the book, but it was hard. The force of what he had released was more powerful than he realized. With all his strength, he slammed it shut and felt a shiver run through his body.

"Walter?" a voice called and he opened his eyes to see starlight above him. Jimmy Alice and Tex knelt over him in the shadowy light of the depot. They helped him up and he stared at them with tears running down his cheeks. Walter launched into Jimmy and Alice's arms. Walter hugged them both, smelling the faint whiff of saltwater in their clothing.

"It's so good to see you again," he cried.

"We've been here all along," Jimmy said, pulling back from Walter's grip with worried eyes. He tilted his head and studied Walter.

"We think you passed out or something," Alice said. "Are you okay?"

"I'm great!" he shouted.

"So, I'm just mincemeat or something, right?" Tex grumbled and Walter was so happy to see him standing there with his red hair reflecting the light and his lopsided smile, he rushed him with a bear hug. Tex patted him on the back and then pushed him back. "People will think we're sweet on each other."

"Where's the book?" Walter asked, looking across the cold grass. Then he stopped. He remembered the book wasn't with them when they arrived here. He had used it to go from the future back in time. Now that he was back in the past, the book was still secured in the chest safe at the hobo jungle where they left it.

"What book?" Alice asked in alarm.

"Nothing," Walter said, shrugging it off.

"Did something happen?" Jimmy asked, catching Walter's arm and making him meet his eyes. Walter let out a sigh of relief.

"No, everything's okay. I must have hit my head when I fell. Going bonkers, I guess."

"You just now figuring that out?" Tex asked. "Okay, let's get going. We gonna hunt us a vamp or not?"

"How can we search the cars with so much activity around here?" Alice whispered.

Jimmy thought about it for a moment, staring at the freighter in front of them. He stuffed the stake into the belt of his overalls and set his face into a grim determination.

"We gotta split up."

"No," Walter snapped and all of them looked at him, startled. "We can't, too many yard bulls around. We need to go up father north and wait for the train to pull out. I know which car the crates are in."

"How would you know a thing like that?" Jimmy asked.

"Just do," Walter mumbled. Jimmy looked at Alice and Tex and shrugged. They all started for the trees, keeping low in the high weeds. Walter eased them into some brush and waited.

"The train's just starting to roll. Alice, this is a double header and it's gonna move fast."

"I'll keep up."

"We'll help," Tex added and Jimmy nodded.

The sleek cars moved down the track toward them, the train whistle haunting the night. Walter waited until enough of the train had passed them, the wheels rolling on the tracks with increasing speed, and he made his move with the rest of them following. They ran alongside the tracks and Walter counted the cars until he saw the one with the Count's crates.

"THAT'S IT!" he screamed, pointing. He made a leap, took the metal rung of the ladder in his hand and swung inside gracefully. He turned and stretched out his hand. Alice ran as fast as she could, her boots slapping against the gravel. Jimmy and Tex were just behind her. Alice's finger's touched Walter's hand and suddenly Tex sprinted ahead of Alice. He threw himself up in the doorway and stuck out his hand. Jimmy took it and slid up into the car. Jimmy and Tex grabbed Walter's coat from behind so he could lean father out and snag Alice's hand in his own. He hoisted her into the train car and she collided into Jimmy, both of them falling on the floor and rolling toward the crates.

"You okay?" Jimmy asked, helping Alice up.

"I'm fine," Alice said. "Thanks, Walter, you really saved my life."

"Not yet," he muttered, "but I will."

"Would you look at all those boxes?"

Alice pulled some candle stubs from her pockets and Tex did the same. They lit them all and the L&N car turned warm in the glow.

"C'mon," Jimmy said, starting to spread out. Walter stopped them.

"No! The book is in that one," he pointed, leaping up on top of a crate and throwing back the lid. His fingers dug through the dirt, sending waves of black soil from the crate to the floor. He hopped down with the leather book secured in his hands. Alice, Tex and Jimmy stared at him with open mouths as he dropped it on the lid of a closed crate and unfastened the buckle.

"Walter?" Alice asked, stepping forward with a cautious half-smile. "How did you know it was up there?"

"Yeah, what gives?" Jimmy added.

Walter looked over with a grim smile. "I think we've been wrong about these books. Bob said if Miss Goode decided to burn the copy of *A Christmas Carol*, he'd never be able to get home, but that's not true. If she destroyed that book, he would stop existing in this world and return to the world inside the pages. I don't think Bob fully understood how much power lies in these things. The books are the key to *everything*. If you destroy the book, you drive the characters back to the printed page where they belong. That's why Miss Goode didn't destroy her version of *A Christmas Carol* after we flew out the window with Santa Claus during the war. It would have been easy, right? But she knew all that would have done was send Bob back where he belonged and she wanted him to suffer. She wanted to squash him between the pages of another book and make him squirm forever."

"Are you sure about this?" Jimmy asked.

"It's the only reason the Count would be ready to kill for it."

"Except he's a monster," Alice countered. "I don't think vampires would go looking for a reason to kill someone."

Walter shook his head and continued. "Why would the Count have this book buried inside the crate? Why was it down inside the dirt? The book needs to rest in that rotting earth sometimes too...just like the Count. It's a part of him. It's all connected. And there's one way to prove it," Walter smiled extending his hand toward Tex. "Give me the stake."

"If I give you the stake, I won't have one."

"You don't need one," Walter huffed. "You're just going to make a mess of things and get yourself thrown off the train. Now hurry!"

"Give it to him!" Alice shouted, and Tex handed over the wooden stake. Walter slipped Tex the crucifix and winked.

"You hold that out in front of him and block his path, so he can't get to Alice or Jimmy. That's very important, okay?"

"Check!"

"He moves fast."

"He's here?"

"*He will be*," Walter whispered, and at that very moment, a scattering of noise slithered overhead. They all looked up.

"He's on the roof," Jimmy whispered.

"I'll get 'im," Tex shouted and started for the train car door, but Alice reached out and pushed him back. The scuttling sound slid over the side of the car and the Count's face peered at them, upside down, from the door. All of them jumped back. His hand curled around the train door and threw it open so hard it slammed into the wall with an earth shattering crash; a cacophony of metal echoed like thunderous heartbeats inside the car. The Count crawled across the ceiling and snarled, leaping to the floor. His lips peeled back to reveal sharp teeth, made even more frightening in the candlelight.

"The crucifix!" Walter shouted. Tex threw out his arm. A glow of white light radiated outward and the vampire hissed, drawing backward with his hands curled into claws, his black overcoat flapping in the wind. The Count lunged to one side and Alice ripped the garlic from around her neck and slapped the monster in the face. He drew back like it was a whip and retreated to the corner of the train car, snarling.

"I know," Walter said in a smug voice, winking at the vampire. The blood red eyes glared at him from a quivering white face of hatred. "Secretly you were hoping I'd come and find you. Well, you won't get my friends this time, you bloodsucker. I have a secret too. You're finished!"

Walter threw open the fine vellum pages of the book and drew the stake back over his head. The vampire screamed, rushing toward Walter in a flurry of dark clothing, but the boy brought his arms down and the stake pierced the pages. The book blossomed into dazzling white light and a rush of warm air filled the train car. If anyone had been looking out a window into the darkness at that moment, as the L&N train was snaking down the tracks, one car would have been covered in dazzling white light. Rays of light shot out through the doorway as if the train car had exploded. A beacon brighter than a lighthouse signal shot up and out into the night with a terrific gust of wind. A moment later and it was over. Walter, Tex, Jimmy and Alice all stood in the cold wind moving through the door and stared at the book. It lay on the floor of the empty train car. The candles had been blown out in the rush of wind, but it was easy to see the crates were gone. The stake still jutted from the smoldering pages of the book.

"Wow," Tex whispered.

They all dropped to the floor and said nothing else until daylight brightened the sky in the east. The double header reached Knoxville, Tennessee and they hopped off. Walter carried the book under his arm. The stake was gone, since they had to rip it free to close the book, but the book was bound tight. Several hobos noticed the group of kids wandering through the switchyards and one even made note of what a strange-looking book they carried. A crucifix was jammed inside the leather binding and a long string of garlic was looped and tied twice around the front. The old hobo found it odd indeed, but said nothing. The children caught a freighter back to Carson Corners while the sun burned bright in the cold October sky.

Chapter Twelve

Our Heroes Return

They arrived at Miss Goode's sprawling mansion on Morton Hill the afternoon of the next day. John was standing on the widow's walk, looking through the witch's telescope with a crowd of monkeys. He saw them coming from two miles off. He let out a whoop, which the winged monkeys imitated, and then he bolted downstairs. He burst into Miss Goode's bedroom, where Bob sat on a cedar chest, having a heart-to-heart conversation with Miss Goode. John told him they were back and zipped down the stairs in a flash. Bob hurried out, leaving Miss Goode still strapped to a chair. They had been letting her use the chamber pot under monkey guard and had been bringing her food and water. Bob had announced that no one would ever be able to say of them they mistreated a kidnapped woman.

Throwing open the door, John leaped from the wide front porch and took off, kicking up a trail of dust on the dirt road. His golden cap still sat perched on his head. A hoard of winged monkeys followed, most of them taking to the air. When John topped the hill, Alice, Tex, Jimmy and Walter all stopped and watched him come yelling over the ridge with a swarm of monkeys darkening the sky like a storm cloud. They all tensed. And then Alice realized her brother was laughing, not screaming. She ran forward, up the hill, until they collided into each other's arms with the monkeys hooting and chattering all around them. Walter, Tex and Jimmy walked up the hill and John hugged each of them while the monkeys flapped overhead.

After a long rest, Bob and Alice fixed a huge meal. Most of it was done with flying monkey assistance. This was not by choice, but because the creatures would not leave them alone. They found everything in the kitchen a wonder. Alice finally had to tell John to make them wait outside, which caused them to swoop around the kitchen windows like oversized bats. The few monkeys that remained in the white-tiled kitchen hopped around, helping stir the batter and light the oven. When Alice would open a cabinet to fetch a plate, a winged monkey was there handing it to her. When she made lemonade, the monkeys wanted to pour the sugar. When she and Bob floured the chicken legs, the monkeys hid in the corner and cowered under the sink. They all knew that chickens were once their fellow creatures with wings. When Alice opened the oven to take out the biscuits, the monkeys stood in awe of the food, their mouths hanging open and steady streams of drool sliding to the floor.

"John?" Walter prodded when they sat down to a feast at Miss Goode's dining room table. John glanced back at the winged monkeys hovering in the doorway, perched on the china cabinet, and lining the stairs with eager eyes.

"You'll get the leftovers," he announced. "Go wait out-side."

A collective groan issued from the winged creatures and they slumped away, but didn't go outside. They only rounded the corner of the dining room and waited, sitting on the floor and grooming each other.

"You think Miss Goode will like the plate we sent up?" John asked and Bob laughed.

"I think the moment we dropped it off, under tight mon-key surveillance, she dove into that plate like a starving wolf. The smells from the kitchen alone are enough to drive anyone mad with hunger."

"Let's pray," Alice said. All of them locked hands and looked around the room. Jimmy squeezed Bob's hand and nodded.

"Why don't you take us through it, Bob?"

"Well, all right." He thought for a moment. "Dear Lord, thank you for guiding us through this nightmare and the horrors we've had to face. We know you were watching out for us in our time of need. Thank you for protecting all of us as we faced great peril and bringing us to this wonderful banquet we can share with the best of friends...no, I take that back. Not friends, but the best *family* anyone could ever want. As my son, Tim, was always fond of saying...God bless us everyone."

Bob raised his head and all of them had tears floating in their eyes. After a few moments of silence, Tex wiped his face on the sleeve of his shirt and puffed out his chest.

"Enough of this sappy stuff, I'm starved!"

He reached for a piece of fried chicken and suddenly

everyone was passing steaming bowls of corn, fried okra, yams, mashed potatoes, ham, biscuits with honey and fresh butter. They stuffed themselves and topped it off with slices of warm apple pie. When they finished, John gave the monkeys the leftovers out back and, for all their usual wild behavior, they sat quietly and ate the remains until their bellies were poking out. Alice and John flopped in a king-sized guest bed. The sheets were soft and the pillows goose down and John fell asleep as his head hit the pillow. His golden cap hung on one of the bedposts, catching odd glints of moonlight. Jimmy and Walter bunked in a spare bedroom down the hall. Bob crawled into a nice soft bed on the third floor with the windows open, letting in cold autumn air. Alice drifted off knowing the house was alive with the sounds of Tex's snoring from the loveseat in the parlor. In the backyard, the monkeys lay stretched out under the stars, belching and passing gas all night.

———

"Double doo-doo," Tex yelled, sprinting into the kitchen where everyone was finishing breakfast. Alice was at the sink washing the dishes and Jimmy was beside her with a dish towel drying and stacking. John was outside in the backyard with the monkeys chattering in the trees. Walter and Bob sat at the pine kitchen table talking. Everything froze as Tex came sliding across the linoleum with panic in his eyes.

"We saved you some eggs," Walter said as Tex stood frozen in panic.

"I forgot about that book you gave me!" he blurted out.

"Everything happened so fast, I plum forgot all about it. That book on *Gunslingers of the Old West* is still in my bindle in the train car."

Alice gave a soft laugh. "Its okay, Tex. We've got to get the other books that we buried under that old Pullman anyway."

"And Tinkerbell," Jimmy added. "C'mon, you and I will go into town and get them."

"Take John," Alice suggested. "He and his monkeys can get you there in a few minutes."

The thick clouds burned away with the sun's heat and Jimmy, Tex and John coasted toward town with Carson Corners dangling below their feet. The largest of the winged monkeys carried John easily, but it took two monkeys each to support Jimmy and Tex. Carson Lake was visible to the east and the small creeks that flowed from the lake ran like tiny blue veins through the lush, green valleys. The clock in the tower of the square was chiming ten as they sailed over Main Street. *Goode's Mercantile* drifted behind them like in a dream and they could see the tracks just over the hill. The tops of the barren trees looked like thin, bony fingers in the cold, bright light of morning. John shouted into the wind, pointing at the shantytowns set up in the field near the tracks, and the monkeys began to drop little by little until Jimmy, Tex and John all touched the earth beneath them.

"I could learn to love that!" Tex panted, his hair blown wild in the wind and his face flushed from the cold.

The largest of the winged monkeys bowed before John, the tip of his misshapen head touching the dirt.

"We need the books." Jimmy nudged John in the arm.

John told the chief monkey where the chest was buried

and asked him to bring Tex's bindle from inside the old train car as well. The huge hairy arms of the beast dangled toward the ground, the knuckles brushing against the dirt as the massive wings lifted him off the ground and over the tracks to the discarded old Pullman. The other monkeys hopped around near John, playing in the dirt and chattering.

"We need to see Old Willie," Tex said, so John commanded the monkeys to remain near the trees while they walked down into the shabby collection of houses. Tex, Jimmy and John strolled in, finding it unusually quiet. Acrid smoke drifted from the garbage cans and a stray bottle rolled in the wind, rattling in its own way against the gravel. Turning a corner, all three of them stopped. Old Willie stood in front of the whole camp of hobos. Most of them had their heads down staring at the earth. Others were looking into the blue sky as if they had lost something there. Old Willie heaved a big sigh and pulled the jar from his pocket. Tinkerbell was still inside. She sat on the bottom of the jar, her soft light visible even in the bright morning sun, and she was tapping one foot impatiently. She was unhurt, but looked perturbed.

Old Willie shuffled his feet. "Hank saw the monkeys in the sky. I know you've come to take her back."

Jimmy reached out and took the glass jar with steady hands.

"I'm sorry, Old Willie, but you can't keep her."

"I know, I know," he mumbled. "I sprinkled a little of that magic powder on some of us last night and we floated for hours. It was the best time I've ever had."

The largest of the winged monkeys came swooping in

with the metal chest under his arm and Tex's bindle under the other. Some of the hobos reacted with shock and stepped back, scared of the dark face that peered at them with huge wings catching the sun's rays. The monkey grunted, his sharp teeth outlined.

"I guess it's time for us to go," John said with a swift nod.

"So long, Old Willie, thanks for your help," Jimmy said. Old Willie nodded and lowered his face. A sniffle followed.

Jimmy caught Tex's arm and stopped in midstep. "Hold up a minute."

Jimmy jumped on a trashcan and hoisted himself on top of the corrugated sheet metal of a makeshift house. He steadied himself and then looked over the pale faces staring up at him and the rows of shanty dwellings. "I guess just one more time wouldn't hurt."

Jimmy shook the jar and spun around, slinging fairy dust out around him. It fell on the housetop and bounced like sparks into the crowd. Old Willie threw back his head, flung out his arms and welcomed it like a spring shower. Slowly and without warning, Old Willie began to hover above the ground. He swung his legs, kicking them wildly as he inched higher. Other hobos were now rising as well. Jimmy sprinkled the dust over Tex and John and over himself. The morning sky was filled with ragged clothes and newspaper-lined boots, dirty faces and the wind at their backs.

"Up, up!" John commanded and the large winged monkey took to the sky with them. The other monkeys in the trees saw them and burst from the branches, soaring and chattering.

"You're angels among men!" Old Willie laughed with his

belly jiggling inside his work shirt. Jimmy, Tex and John started home with the monkeys flapping along beside them and the hobos went swimming through the morning light like dark swans in a vast, blue sea.

Alice had finished cleaning up and Bob had gone outside to sit on the porch after their large breakfast. Walter helped Alice clear the rest of the table. He looked down the long hallway and could see a patch of sky and grass, darkened by the screen door to a dirty gray, but at least it was there. He realized how close all of them had come to never seeing a blue sky or sunlight again.

"Thinking you should have gone?" Alice asked, noticing his stare.

"Nah, they can handle it."

"I don't think we did such a good job of handling it the other night."

Walter glanced at her and he cast his eyes downward. He dropped into a chair and draped his elbow over the back. "You know something happened, right? Something bad?"

Alice walked over and stood by the table's edge. Soft sunlight slipped through the lace curtains over the sink. "When you raised that stake over your head, you looked at the Count and said something about 'you're not going to get my friends this time.' What did you mean?"

Walter took in a deep breath and told Alice everything. She slipped into a chair beside him and listened without interrupting. The weight of what happened hit her hard.

"So, Jimmy and Tex and I died that night?"

Walter nodded. Alice ran her fingers along the tabletop. "It's funny, but I have no memory of it."

"Because it didn't happen. I changed it."

"And Bob was going to give up going back to his world for you and John? He was going to stay and take care of you?"

Walter nodded. Alice reached over and kissed him on the cheek.

"That was a brave thing you did, Walter. You saved all our lives."

"You would have done the same," he said and she smiled. The remaining monkeys began squawking from the trees out back, signaling the return of the others. Alice and Walter went outside, the screen door slamming behind them as they watched the dark shapes come sailing closer and closer along the treetops, until there were three boys and a small group of winged monkeys on the horizon.

"There they are now." Bob laughed, standing up and stretching. Alice walked over and put her arm around Bob and squeezed. He smiled and kissed the top of her head.

Chapter Thirteen

Α Witch's Ruse, Ruckus & Revenge

"Okay, Miss Goode, we need answers," Alice announced, looking down at her. She sat in the huge golden chair, still bound tight as the late morning light came shifting into the room. After recovering the books, they had all marched into her bedroom where rose-print wallpaper adorned the room and priceless antiques filled the corners. Alice nodded and Jimmy removed the scarf from her mouth. The witch shifted her jaw and then her lips formed a thin, hard line. She looked up, facing Alice, while the others stood in the background. "We need the other books, the ones you've had in your possession all these years and you're the only one who knows where they are."

Miss Goode smacked her lips and then grinned. She stayed silent.

"We've taken care of everything else—"

"We hope," Jimmy interjected.

"—and now we need to undo some of the mess you've made with people's lives. All those employees down at your store want to go home. If you tell us where the books are, we won't send you back to Oz—unless that's where you want to go. But we have a yard full of winged monkeys," she groaned, rolling her eyes. "We need to send them back, and you have the copy of *The Wonderful Wizard of Oz*. John is keeping the cap here in this world with us, no matter what. Those monkeys will not be your slaves again, but we need to return them to the book. We've already dropped Tinkerbell back into Never Never Land. We decided to leave Santa Claus here. We thought the world might be a better place with him in it."

"C'mon," Walter urged. "You have the chance to do something good for some people."

Miss Goode nodded and shifted her black eye over, watching them all with a steady gaze.

"Very well," she whispered. "Untie me and I'll show you where they are."

"Tell us where they are first," Tex snapped back. "Then we'll untie you."

"In that closet," she said, nodding across the room. "There is a false wall in the back. You open it by twisting the sconce on the wall to the left."

Jimmy, Tex and Walter ran over and threw open the closet door. It was musty and smelled of mothballs and old linen. Walter took hold of the stone sconce on the wall outside the closet and turned it to the left. The back wall inside the closet slid aside with a groan. Jimmy grabbed a candle and lit the wick. All three of them entered the small room that had been revealed. Alice and Bob both ventured over after a moment with John trailing behind them. It was a tiny room, with no windows, and it was empty. They all stood looking around, bumping into each other and hitting their heads on low beams in the vaulted ceiling. Alice emerged from the stuffy room and the others followed. Miss Goode looked smug and happy.

"There's nothing in there."

The witch chuckled. "Oh yes, there is. It's protected though."

"Protected?"

"I'm the only one who can remove the spell."

"Do it," Tex demanded. Miss Goode rolled her black eye back in her head.

"I have a few conditions. I'll give you what you want, if you give me what I want."

"What's that?" Jimmy asked. They all stood silent while she cleared her throat and then let out a sigh.

"First of all, I want to keep some of the books—"

"No way, sister!" Tex shouted.

"You didn't let me finish, little troll," she grumbled and John, Tex and Bob all took a step back. "I'll keep only two or three and you can be the judge of how harmless they are."

"It's too dangerous," Alice countered. "I'm sorry, Miss Goode, but no one can keep the books. We're going to hide them somewhere so that no one will ever be able to get them again."

"Like I did?" she asked. Her eye pivoted to the left and glared at Alice. "I dropped the ones I couldn't use in a hole and look what happened! Years later, those lousy books wouldn't stay buried. They stirred and shifted and called until someone answered. You think you can actually put them somewhere *safe*?"

"We have a way to transport them to a place where they can't hurt anyone ever again. I got the idea when we fought Moby Dick. He swallowed it. Everything went back to the way it was before he'd been released, but the book was still gone. It got me thinking we could haul the books all into *one* book and then take that one and keep it safe forever."

"You foolish little girl...it doesn't work that way. You'd have to convince a character to do this for..." her voice trailed off when she saw Bob smiling in the background. He shrugged. "Oh I see. Bob Crachit is going to take them all into the pages of Dickens. Then what? What if Ebenezer Scrooge decides he wants to open the books and see what horrors can be unleashed on London?"

"It's not written that way, so it can't happen," Walter said. Miss Goode threw back her head and let out a scream. She struggled against the chair and twisted inside the ropes that pinned her arms and legs. She tired herself out, her hair hanging in disarray across her forehead. Huffing out great mouthfuls of air, she curled her fingers into claws and clutched the golden armrests.

Bob stepped up. "You know this is for the best, Effigy. I can take all the books into that world and no one will ever be able to open them. The characters only have free will in this world, not the world of the written page. And what if someone did find my copy of *A Christmas Carol*? What's the worst that could happen? Ebenezer Scrooge before his Christmas Eve transformation would be a miserly old gent at his very worst. The ghosts of Christmas Past, Present and

Future could be a blessing for stingy people around the holidays, showing them a path toward mercy. You see? We've worked it all out."

"*I'll never release the spell*," she hissed. "When I get loose, I'll have you all thrown in prison! You'll spend your days hammering on a chain gang!"

She sat back and fumed in silence. Alice looked over at Jimmy and he shrugged. They all stepped to the door and huddled between the hallway and the bedroom. They kept their voices low.

"What do we do now?" John asked.

"Wicked don't do her justice," Tex snarled. "She's a stubborn old girl for sure. If she won't give up the books, let's have those monkeys tear this place apart."

"She said it's a spell," Alice reminded him. "They could be in that small room off from the closet and we can't see them because they're enchanted."

"I think she's bluffing," Walter suggested.

Bob nodded. "Yes, I do too. Her powers are very limited in this world because all the spells, charms and magic weapons were probably left in Oz. She *could* have brought them with her, but things that might have seemed like magic in Oz, might not be as powerful here in this world. It's like a piece of silver that's tarnished. It's been so many years maybe the shine has worn off."

"Well, I got a solution," Tex announced. "We let the monkeys have their way with her. If they scratch and bite her enough, maybe she'll holler mercy and give up."

"Would you leave those monkeys out of this," Walter groaned.

Bob continued. "I think she wants us to let her go, but she has no intention of showing us where the books are located. A hidden room off the closet may be just that and nothing more. Those books are going to be impossible to find."

"We can't keep her tied up forever," Jimmy said.

"Okay, we'll untie her, but be ready for anything," Alice moaned.

They all wandered back into the bedroom. Miss Goode stared off into space, pretending that she had not been trying to listen. Alice walked over.

"We're going to let you go, but only to show us where the books are, and that's it. When we have them safe and sound, we'll finish up and you're free to go."

"You're forgetting, dear," she smiled sweetly, "this is my house. When we're finished, *you're* free to go. I'll want you out of my house, out of this town. Good riddance."

Jimmy and Tex pulled the knots free and Miss Goode stood up, wobbling on shaky legs. She regained her balance and stretched. The tattered folds of her pink nightgown were covered in dried mud. She swept her hands along her face, pulling her hair back.

"After being strapped down there for almost two days, I'm a little stiff."

"The spell?" Jimmy indicated, pointing toward the closet.

"It takes concentration…and privacy."

"We're not leaving you alone," Walter said.

Tex stepped up and winked. "And if you try anything funny, we're not opposed to giving you a knuckle sandwich."

"Such charm," Miss Goode grumbled while rolling her eye. "Very well, but you'll have to step back out of the way.

The magic is old. I didn't bring it with me from Oz. It came from another volume."

"By the way, where did the books come from?" Walter asked. Miss Goode glanced over, readjusting her eye patch.

"I don't know. I came out of the book into this world and all I could ever discover was that the real Effigy Goode must have come into possession of them and didn't realize their awesome power. She was unprepared for characters to come from the page into existence. It was quite a shock for her."

"Where is she?" Alice asked.

Miss Goode gritted her yellowing teeth. "She was a necessary loss."

"You killed her?" John asked with disbelief in his eyes.

"She had released several key characters without knowing it. I helped her secure them back into the books and I made sure she went with them. Poor thing never knew what hit her. She was here one moment, gone the next...sucked into a vortex of white light. I moved here to Carson Corners after assuming her identity."

"So you left her in a book?" Alice asked.

"It was a nice story," Miss Goode answered with indignation. "A lovely novel you might have heard of called *Treasure Island*. She's been living it up on an exotic island in the middle of the deep blue sea for the past thirty years. That much I did for her, so stop gawking at me as if I'm some monster."

"How did my mother not know?" Alice asked, more to herself than as a direct question. Miss Goode laughed.

"They had not seen each other in awhile and when I assumed her identity, I made sure to sever all ties with the family. Your mother wrote to me, of course, and I always wrote back telling her I never wanted to see her again. I made up some story about our parents always favoring her. Finally, I stopped answering the letters all together."

"Okay," Jimmy said. "Break the spell and get us the books so we can free Alice and John's real aunt and get Bob back home."

"All right," she whispered. "I'll need some things from the kitchen, fresh water pumped from the well for scrying. Make sure it's in a medium-sized bowl. I'll need salt, garlic gloves, an onion and a jar of canned tomatoes from the cellar."

"We'll get it," Jimmy and Walter said together, running from the room.

"Next," she announced, "I'll need candles."

Alice nodded thoughtfully and began lighting the candles, which sat in silver holders by the bedside, on the mahogany chest of drawers and by the unused fireplace along the wall.

"I hope you don't mind, but I'd like to freshen up just a moment. Can someone take me to the washroom?"

"Come along," Bob waved and they stepped from the bedroom into the dark hallway. The stained glass window by the stairs allowed a multitude of colors to reflect across the upstairs hardwood floor. Miss Goode stepped into her powder room and Bob stood just outside the door, watching as she took out her hairbrush and began running it through the tangles. Miss Goode opened her medicine cabinet and took down some makeup and began applying it generously around her cheeks. She twisted a tube of bright red lipstick at the base and touched the tip to her mouth. She smacked her lips and then dabbed with a tissue to remove the excess.

Bob stuffed his hands in his pockets. He could hear Jimmy and Walter downstairs rummaging through the kitchen. Miss Goode approached the door and winced. "Robert, this is a bit embarrassing. I need to use the little girl's room. Do you mind if I close the door for a moment?"

"That's not a good idea. I'll have Alice come in there with you."

"Oh honestly, Robert," she sighed. "The window is only a foot tall. I couldn't get through it if I tried, and where would I go even if I did miraculously squeeze through? I think it's safe to let me use the powder room in peace."

"All right, I'll pull the door a little, but you can't shut it all the way."

"Fair enough," she conceded. Miss Goode pushed the door halfway closed and Bob glanced down the hallway. The bedroom was aglow with candlelight. He stepped over and leaned against the banister. His gaze shifted and he realized that, from where he stood, he had a full view of Miss Goode in the large mirror on the wall above the sink. *At least I can still keep an eye on her,* he thought, even though the embarrassment made his face flush. He realized she had turned around and was facing the mirror. He could see her staring at her reflection and then her good eye shifted in the glass and caught him watching her. Bob started to look away, but she began to smile—a dark, greedy, hungry smile. Those bright red lips were stretched wide and her teeth seemed to sparkle in the bathroom's white glow.

"Gotcha," she hissed in an angry voice. She turned in a

flash, slamming the door and turning the key in the lock.

"ALICE!" Bob screamed, throwing himself against the wood of the door and jiggling the knob. He could hear footsteps in the bedroom and then pounding down the hallway behind him. Bob turned his shoulder and slammed it against the door, but it wouldn't budge. Alice, John and Tex were right beside him. A barrage of questions came out of nowhere:

"What happened?"

"Where is she?"

"Is she in there?"

"She's locked herself in," Bob shouted. "It was all a trick."

Jimmy and Walter came racing up the second landing and stood in shock. They ran down the hallway and dumped everything they were carrying on the floor. After Bob explained what had happened, Jimmy, Tex, Walter and Bob all drew back and, on the count of three, hurled themselves at the doorway. They bounced off the door and stumbled in the hall.

"It must be reinforced or something," Jimmy said, rubbing his shoulder.

"Effigy!" Bob shouted and then listened at the door. She was moving around inside, but he couldn't tell what she was doing. There was a clattering noise and then footsteps across the tile. "Effigy, can you hear me? We're not going to hurt you. Jimmy and Walter brought everything you required to break the spell."

"You simple snot," she raged from behind the door. They all jumped at her fury. "There was never any spell!"

"I knew it!" Walter stomped his foot.

Bob let out a long sigh. "But what about all these things you wanted from the kitchen?"

"It's the ingredients for tomato soup. Fire up the stove and make a nice pot. Enjoy! My plan was to get you scattered and for me to get in here."

"Why?" Alice shouted.

"Don't you know?" she giggled from the other side.

They all looked at each other. Collectively they said, "*The books.*"

"That's right," Miss Goode shrieked. "They were tucked away safe and sound in my bathroom! Thought you could outsmart me, huh? Well, you're nothing more than ill-mannered, poorly educated little gutter rats!"

"John," Alice called. "Get the monkeys, quick."

———

Inside the bathroom, Miss Goode pressed a hidden lever under the sink. A section of tile wall popped back. She crossed the floor and stooped down, drawing back the door with a hidden handle. The books sat stacked on two shelves inside the wall, overflowing. She'd never been hard-pressed enough to put anything in that old storage room off her closet, but it had been her ticket! She had gotten them this time. Pressing a long, thin finger to her pouty red lips, she stared at the books and mused. Which one would do the trick? She snatched a copy or two, scanned the titles and tossed them back inside with no concern. Most of the ones she had kept for herself involved the employees at the store, but a few were important to her, of course. The copy of *The Wonderful Wizard of Oz* was there, and a well-used copy of

Treasure Island. It had come in handy when she learned how the books really worked. She had imprisoned poor Effigy Goode, the real one, somewhere on Treasure Island...after young Jim Hawkins had hauled Long John Silver's gold from the pages into this world. Little Jim had gone into the books for her and brought out untold amounts of gold doubloons. He was a simple boy and when she had sent him back into the pages, she made sure the real Effigy went with him. She had heard someone knocking against the cover and scratching at the pages, especially late in the night, but it finally went away after a year or so. Now, she was a rich and prosperous woman, with a thriving business even in such dark financial times, and she planned to keep it that way.

She had heard those blasted children yelling from the other side of the door, but now there was a great commotion in the hallway. She paused and listened, then heard hundreds of tiny fingers trying to claw their way in. *The winged monkeys,* she thought. Of course! It had been a mistake to bring them from Oz, but she had underestimated those children. Once they got the cap and learned it was the only way to control the monkeys, she had lost the upper hand. Now she had it back. Ten years ago, fearing someone might try to get to the books, she had the door reinforced with a steel frame. They would be banging on the door and trying to get in until doomsday if she wanted. And when she'd found the perfect method to send them all somewhere safe, she'd open the door and play the frail old woman. 'Oh, don't hurt me.'

Now she needed to release something into this world that she could send back without a lot of fuss. And when the time came, she'd be sure to gather those little darlings up

In the folds. Their lives would be lived between the book covers, watching the words unfold before them, but never able to change or effect the lives around them, a kind of living death. *Ahhhhh*, she thought, pulling a battered copy from the pile and giving it the once-over with a steady eye. *They are children after all and need something adventurous. I have the perfect thing. It will keep them entertained for years.* She unbuckled the strap of *1001 Arabian Nights* and opened the book. Miss Goode rubbed the pages and a pale pink mist emerged, sliding up the walls and filling the room with the scents of ancient spices: patchouli, sandalwood, cinnamon. *I should have thought of this in the first place*, she rattled in her mind, *instead of releasing those stupid monkeys.*

Her eye snapped up and she saw the cursed little monkey faces at the small window. One of them shrieked and hissed, its tiny fangs catching the light. They were banging on the glass and would smash it open soon. If even one of them got in, it would unlock the door for the others. She felt a sense of panic. She rubbed faster and the mist grew thicker, swirling inside the bathroom with colors and shapes like cloud formations. *Hurry*, she thought.

All of them stood out of the way as the monkeys swarmed in a mass of wings and fur, clamoring at the door and the frame. Several of them were gnawing at the hinges while others had punched small holes in the wall trying to rip through. All of their wings had generated a furious wind rushing through the hallway. Alice looked over at Jimmy with worried eyes.

"She's up to no good! We've got to get in there now!" she shouted over the shrill monkey cries.

"Faster monkeys, faster!" John yelled.

"Maybe we—" Jimmy started and then everything went silent. The wind and chattering died, and they all stood in the shadowy hallway with their mouths hanging open. The monkeys were gone. One moment they had been there and the next, only the scratches on the door and the damage to the walls remained. John ran over and put his hand on the door, his small fingers tracing the deep scratches with a cry in his throat.

"My monkeys," he said, turning and looking at everyone. His hand went to his head and the golden cap was gone. His blond hair was flattened to his head after wearing the cap for days. Tears crept into his eyes. "What'd she do to them?"

"C'mere." Alice motioned with her hand. Curls of pale pink smoke moved from under the door. He bolted to his sister's side and they all stepped back. The smoke rose and floated in the air like snakes. They heard the lock being turned and the door to the bathroom opened with a brief gust of wind and smoke. Alice held her breath and felt Jimmy's hand on her arm. Tex made a strange noise in his throat and Bob and Walter were as silent as church mice.

Miss Goode stepped through the haze of smoke in her tattered pink nightgown. Her makeup was thick and her bright red lipstick was almost visible before she was, but then her ghastly face followed out of the smoke. She curled her fingers together over an opened book, crushing it to her chest.

"What did you do with my monkeys?" John yelled. When his voice had died, the echo lingering on the stairwell, Miss

Goode laughed a deep, throaty laugh.

"I sent them back where they belonged. In hindsight, it was a mistake to bring them here at all. They are a formidable army, but controlled only by that golden cap. I had plenty of other minions I should have released—wolves or crows or bees. They would have been better, I think."

"What now?" Jimmy asked.

"What now?" Miss Goode repeated in a sinister voice. "Well, I have released something with infinitely more power that has to obey my every whim. Let me show you what I mean. I don't want their feet to move from that spot."

The swirling mist floated out from the bathroom on its own, drifting upward and forming what looked like a face. They all could see it. Two slanted dark eyes floated before them and a long black beard had become visible. A second later, they could see the man's features even more clearly.

"As you command," a voice rumbled and the house shook on its foundation.

"Hey!" Tex tried to move, but he tilted left and right and then collapsed backward. His knees bent and his backside hit the hardwood floor with a smack. All of them found the same thing had happened. Their feet just below the ankles would not leave the floor. It was as if some great magnet had anchored them. Alice fell over, followed by Walter and Bob. John and Jimmy stuck their arms out for balance and remained standing.

"It's a genie," Walter yelled. "She's conjured a genie from a book to do her bidding.

"Guilty as charged," the witch laughed. "Just opened the book and rubbed the pages and, *viola!*"

"If she used a wish to send the monkeys back and a wish to nail us to the floor, she only has one left."

"Don't worry…I only need one more wish and I'll make it a *good* one."

"How can you be so nasty?" John yelled. She walked over and grabbed his right earlobe in her nails, squeezing tight enough to draw a drop of blood.

"How can you be so *stupid*?"

"You're ugly!" he fired back.

"You're a sore loser."

"Leave him alone," Alice shouted, trying to twist around on the floor, but her feet would not respond. She grunted, trying to stand up, but couldn't get her balance. She fell back down with a plop. Reaching over, she picked up the closest thing to her, the jar of tomatoes Jimmy and Walter had brought up. She threw it at Miss Goode, but missed. It sailed through the pink smoke and smashed along the back wall. "He's just a little boy!"

"But he's not very good at being one, is he?" Miss Goode growled, staring at the tomato juice running down the wall. "You will all go back into the book with the genie, but I'm thinking my last wish should have something to do with this little brat. I think he should stay here and be my little helper. He can be my mute…little…monkey!"

"No!" Alice screamed. "You can take me instead of him."

"I don't want you, dear," she hissed.

"But John can't do anything. He can't cook. He's too lazy to clean up properly. He's only nine years old!"

"I'll train him well."

"He won't be any good to you."

"Take me," Jimmy said. "I can cook a little and I'll work real hard for you, Miss Goode. Take me instead of him."

"No, take me!" Tex bellowed.

"I'll stay!" Walter shouted.

"SHUT UP!" Miss Goode raged. "It's all very noble, but I'm not taking any of you except this scruffy little mongrel."

"Effigy," Bob began, "he's just a child. None of them knew anything about your involvement with the books until I told them. Do you hear me? I was the one who told them. If there is someone you wish to punish, take your wrath out on me."

"Hush up, Bob. You're a good accountant, but a lousy martyr. This dirty little brat will be mine and there's nothing that will change that. He'll make such a good little chimp, especially without a tongue."

A thought suddenly occurred to Alice. Not so much a thought, as a memory. It slipped into her mind like sinking into a warm winter coat on a snowy day. Alice shifted her eyes around her. The hallway shadows were thick and brown, but she found what she was looking for and smiled.

"Besides," Alice announced in a light voice, "even if you turn him into a mute little monkey, he'll still be prettier than you."

A long silence filled the hallway and Miss Goode released John's ear. She stalked over and stared down at Alice with her one good eye. Her lips pulled back from her teeth in a snarl.

"You're a savvy one, but 'me thinks thou dost protest too much'. You see, it'll be far greater revenge to have him here until the end of his days, waiting on me hand and foot. You'll be trapped—forever, I might add—inside the book and little John will grow up and grow old spending his years in servitude. I think I'll put him in a velvet blazer with tiny brass buttons and a cap with a tassel like you see in paintings from Cairo. Maybe a ribbon in his tail? Doesn't that sound sweet?"

"I read your book," Alice said, her fingers inching along the baseboard. Miss Goode was startled from her reverie with a frown.

"What?"

"My mom read it to me every night when I was little. We read the whole series together. I loved it."

"So?"

"Maybe you should have stayed there."

Miss Goode laughed. "You're a strange little girl. You remind me of Dorothy Gale in an odd way. She was another irritable, meddling little snot, did you know that?"

"I learned a thing or two from her," Alice whispered. She slid the ceramic bowl into her palm. Cupping her hand around the bowl, she heaved it forward and splattered Miss Goode in the face with the water. A horrid shriek reverberated along the upstairs landing. Miss Goode dropped the book on Alice's leg and lurched back with her hands covering her face. Thin trails of steam leaked from between her fingers, her skin started to blister and burn. A horrid smell like burnt cabbage floated into the hallway and everyone started gagging and coughing. Miss Goode fell against the back wall and slid down into tomato juice and broken glass, still screaming. Her pink nightgown bubbled as if made of tar.

Moments passed and, when the shrieks began to fade,

they all looked up and saw a brown bubbling mass of goo in the hallway. Her pink nightgown was still there, but Miss Goode was gone. Smoke floated upward and evaporated into the air.

"Holy cow," Tex uttered through numb lips. "Is that what happened in the book?"

"Yep," Alice smiled.

Tex snorted. "They ought to make a picture show out of that."

Alice scooted the copy of *1001 Arabian Nights* forward until she could touch the pages. Looking up at the genie hovering in his pink fog, she saw that he was expressionless. Alice closed the book and then rubbed it with her fingers. She opened it again and looked up with an uncertain face. "Do you have to obey me now?"

"Yes, mistress. You are granted three wishes," he roared, and the walls shook with his booming roar.

"Undo whatever you did so we can stand up, all right?"

"Done," he thundered and Alice, Walter, Bob and Tex stood up. They braced themselves on one leg and wiggled one foot and then did likewise with the other one. John ran over and hugged Alice around the waist. Jimmy stepped from the spot where he was anchored and heaved a sigh of relief.

"The books," Bob said and they all ran into the bathroom. The wall door was still open and they sat down on the cool tiles and began pouring through the leather-bound copies. As they raked the books off the shelves, they realized how deep the cupboard really was–there were bags of gold behind the books. The genie followed them in, floating on a thin pink wave of mist.

"We can do this quick," Tex said, hooking his thumb over his shoulder at the genie. "This big lug could make everything right in a snap."

Alice sighed in relief and they all looked at each other with wide smiles.

"Okay," Alice agreed and made her second wish. The genie waved his hands and a bolt of thunder echoed somewhere outside. John ran downstairs and threw open the door. A pause followed and then he yelled from the porch.

"They're here!"

Walking downstairs with Jimmy, Tex, Walter and Bob toting the books, Alice found all the employees–characters Miss Goode had dragged from the pages and then blackmailed into working for her—standing on the stoop. They all looked dazed and uncertain at their sudden change of surroundings. Alice stepped up and began explaining the situation. When they heard Miss Goode was gone a cheer erupted from the group of twenty or so people. Alice explained that everyone who wanted to go back into the books could have the opportunity. A murmur floated through the group, and then the lady John and Alice had met the first day in town stepped forward.

"I want to go home," she said with a sigh, tears forming in her eyes. She kissed John and Alice both and thanked them and then she was gone. A flash of light, a rush of heat across the porch, and Anne had gone back to Green Gables. One by one, they stepped up, some to go home and some to stay behind. Some of them had found they enjoyed being free. Others had married or had children in the time they had spent outside the pages.

"Howdy." A fresh-faced man appeared. He had freckles dotting his nose and rocked back and forth on his heels as he scratched his head. "I've been thinking this here thing over and I'm pretty sure I'd rather have the adventures I was meant to have. It's been swell here and all, but can you send me back?"

"Of course," Walter said and Alice held out *The Adventures of Huckleberry Finn*. The man with the boyish face stepped up and smiled.

"Never thought I'd get the chance to go back. It's a strange world, ain't it?"

He gave a sharp nod at them and put his hand on the open pages. He was gone in a flash. Alice closed the book and handed it to Walter for buckling. By late afternoon, everyone was gone. Those who returned to the books were safe inside the pages and those who wanted to remain in this world had walked down the road back into town, free to live their own lives without Miss Goode's form of slavery.

"That was some fancy footwork this morning," Jimmy said to Alice, sitting on the front porch of Miss Goode's massive house as twilight darkened the sky. "If you hadn't thrown that bowl of water at her, we'd have been toast."

She looked over and smiled.

"I just remembered what was already written, that's all. We came real close to getting stomped...again."

"I know," he nodded and then did a doubletake. "Again? You mean the whale?"

"Dracula," she sighed. Alice told him everything that Walter had related to her in the kitchen that morning. Jimmy sat staring at her with his mouth hanging open.

"You and Tex died and I got bit?" he asked, instinctively reaching up and rubbing his fingers along his throat.

"Yeah, pretty scary stuff, huh?"

Jimmy tried to take it all in, but one image came creeping back to haunt him. If he had been bitten by the vampire he might have become one too. He imagined himself rising up from the dirt under an abandoned train yard at night to hunger after human blood. He felt goose bumps running up and down his arms. Jimmy shook the thought away. Walter opened the screen door and poked his head out, pushing his glasses back up the bridge of his nose.

"There you two are. Come on inside. We got some stuff to talk about."

Jimmy stopped at the doorway and put a hand on Walter's arm. "Thanks, pal."

"For what?"

"You know." Jimmy prodded and Walter could see in Jimmy's eyes that Alice had told him everything. He shrugged.

"I just thought about what you would do, Jim. You never stop...never quit. I kept repeating that over and over."

"I'm mighty glad you did," he smiled. They walked inside and found everyone gathered in the parlor. They stood in the doorway, arms crossed. Walter had all the books sitting on the floor or stuffed in the metal chest sitting to the side. John sat cross-legged on the floor, picking at the corner of *The Wonderful Wizard of Oz*. Alice rolled her eyes and shook her head. John mouthed the word *please*. She shook her head harder.

"C'mon," he said out loud.

"No," she said. "Those monkeys can't come back and stay your friends forever. They belong in Oz and that's where they have to stay."

He huffed and dropped his head.

Alice glanced over at her third wish.

Her real aunt sat in a white linen dress on the loveseat. Her brown hair was piled on top of her head and a string of pearls hung around her pale throat. She was still trying to comprehend everything they had told her. The genie had released her from the book in a flash and suddenly she had been in front of them, a girl of no more than eighteen, who had been trapped in a book for almost thirty years. Alice walked over and sat beside her, holding her hand.

"Are you all right?"

"It's kind of a blur," her aunt said, shaking her head. "I remember being somewhere warm and there was a stretch of coastline. I think there were pirates. I don't know how I got there—or how I got here, for that matter. I see words in my head, running over and over again."

"Maybe it's better if you don't remember much about what happened." Alice comforted her. "The important thing is that you're here with us. Tex went into town today for us and sent a wire to mama and papa. They should be here in a few days. Mama has changed, she's gotten older, but she'll be so happy to see you again."

Aunt Effigy nodded, her pretty lips curving into a delicate smile.

"I like her better than the other one," Tex announced with a wink. His cheeks blushed a fiery red. "I hope I worded that telegraph okay."

Alice looked over with her eyes growing wide. "I thought you told me you put down for them to come as quick as possible and we would explain later."

"It was something like that." Tex shuffled his feet. "I might have added a little bit about Miss Goode going up in smoke and your real aunt coming back from *Treasure Island*."

"Oh good gravy," Jimmy said, slapping his forehead. "I told you I should have done it."

"Maybe they'll come even faster with a message like that," John giggled.

"Well," Bob announced, standing up and straightening his jacket. "I suppose it's time for me to go. We sent the genie back into the dark of an Arabian night and the books are here, all accounted for and tightly secured. I can take them with me as planned."

"You don't have to go," Alice said. "Someone else can let the genie free and we'll get three more wishes. We can have these books sent to another dimension where no one can get them. You can stay with us."

"No, we've misused these books too much already. Besides, there's nothing left for me to do here."

"That's not true," Walter protested.

"Yes, I'm afraid it is, lad. Alice and John have their real aunt back with them. She'll be better soon and their whole family will come to live here. The store is still a thriving place of business in this town. There are a few repairs that need to be made, but all of you can handle that. I did her ledgers, so, believe me, I know all-too-well how much money that store brings in every month. And you and Jimmy and

Tex can go anywhere you want, Walter. We found the Wicked Witch's stash of gold with the books. Divided between you three and Alice and John, you'll all be set for life."

"You don't have to leave," Walter continued. "You told me once it was better to be real than fiction."

"Did I?" he questioned. His thick white eyebrows inched together and his eyes flickered off in thought.

"Well," Walter started, forgetting that Bob had told him that before he had changed time. After Walter reversed events, Bob never really said it at all. "What I mean is...that sounds like something you would have said."

"Yes, it does, you're right about that, but I have to go back and live the life that was written for me."

"Will you remember us?" Alice asked. Bob tilted his head and smiled.

"How could I ever forget you? I'll keep the memories deep inside."

"I feel like I'm gonna cry," Alice said, standing and wrapping her arms around Bob's neck. Walter and Jimmy joined in. John leaped from the floor and clung to Bob's leg. Tex shrugged and slung his arms around them too.

"I'm not sure what all this is about, but I feel like I'm going to cry too," Aunt Effigy said sniffling from the loveseat. Tex pulled a handkerchief from his back pocket and handed it to her.

"All right," Bob sighed. He stepped back with a tight smile. He wiped away the tears and looked at the leather book on the coffee table. "I guess this is it. Walter, will you do the honors? Open the book and then stand back."

Walter unbuckled the strap and tossed it open. The pages

had a sweet smell of Christmas to them: cooked turkey and pudding. A tinkle of music floated in the wind. Bob knelt down and gathered all the books near him. He made sure his foot was touching the metal trunk and his left hand was on the stack of books they had found upstairs in the bathroom. He looked up and made eye contact with them all.

"It's been thirty years since I've been there. To be honest, I'm a little nervous. I'll go back to being a young man again with a family. Belinda and Martha will be there, the twins. Peter, my oldest son will be ready to be apprenticed. Five-and-sixpence weekly, I believe he'll be earning. My wife, dressed in her twice-turned gown and ribbons. And Tim."

"'Who did not die'," Walter quoted from Dickens classic. Bob nodded.

"That's right. You keep this copy safe. If you ever need me, just open the pages and call my name. It might take me awhile, but I'll find my way back out. It's been quite an adventure and I'm so happy to have known you. I love you all," he stammered, hot tears running down his cheeks. Bob dropped his hand against the pages and light as bright as the midday sun blasted through the parlor. Aunt Effigy was caught by surprise and screamed. A hot wind barreled through the room and Alice opened her eyes as the light faded. Bob and the books were gone. The copy of *A Christmas Carol* lay on the coffee table, the pages still drifting in some strange wind. Walter stepped over to close it, sniffling, trying to hold back the tears. A piece of holly had materialized from the pages of the book, like some buoyant piece of cork floating to the surface of a pond. He handed it to Alice and she pressed it to her nose. The smell was strong and the leaves were cold and crisp from winter wind. The bright red berries still had a few stray snowflakes on them that were just starting to melt. Walter shut the book and slid the strap through the buckle. They were all silent.

Chapter Fourteen

What Happened Afterward?

hen John and Alice's parents arrived from Alabama, they hopped off the train a mile from the station, just as the cars began to slow down. They walked through the high grass with other hobos toward the depot. From a distance they saw Alice and John leaping through the weeds with smiles on their faces, and then both Eunice and Carl Horton were knocked flat by their children. Both parents fell to the grass while Alice and John kissed them and held tight. Eunice was amazed to see her children so properly clean. Alice had her hair down and a pretty yellow dress on. John, in a clean cotton shirt and jeans, bounced around the fields shouting, "We're the Book Battling Kids!" Eunice stopped listening and went into mild shock when the children crawled into the interior of the 1931 sedan parked by the station. Tex saluted them from the driver's seat and popped the thing in gear, the motor humming like a prowling tiger. Having driven everything from horses to tractors, he was having the time of his life behind the wheel. The day was colder and stray pumpkins, abandoned after Halloween, sat on front porches near the depot as the two parents slid into the smooth, cool interior.

Eunice and Carl listened very intently to the story Alice and John unfolded and, by the time they had reached the huge mansion on the hill, they were staring open-mouthed in full-fledged disbelief. Walter and Jimmy were standing on the porch in dress slacks and pinstriped shirts when they arrived. Jimmy thumped Walter on the arm and they ran down the steps, opened the car doors and shook hands enthusiastically with both Carl and Eunice Horton. Alice could tell her parents didn't quite believe everything they were being told, but when Eunice saw her sister, Effigy, who was still only a slip of a girl, no more than eighteen, they must have accepted the gravity of what had happened— even if it never made sense.

As the months wore on, Alice was never sure if her parents really believed them or not, but over time it became less important. A small brass plaque outside the doors of the renamed *Horton and Goode's Mercantile* read: **Permanently Under New Management.** Alice and Jimmy married eight years later and stayed in the house with the family after their honeymoon. When their first child, Robert, was born followed by Anne two years later, they moved over to a quaint two-story house on Ridgecrest to be closer to the store. John went off to college and became a veterinarian. Tex and Walter never hit the rails again. In time, Walter took over as head librarian of the Carson Corners Memorial Library. For years he woke in a sweat from nightmares; *Dracula* was the only book strictly forbidden from the shelves of the library. His poor eyesight kept him from going to war. Since Jimmy's hearing in his left ear was never the same after the encounter with Moby Dick, he stayed home too. Tex returned from World War II a local hero who earned a purple heart, the flying cross and two air metals. His B25 bomber had been called *The Book Battling Kids.* The guys in his unit kidded him about it. They would always ask just what the heck a Book Battling Kid was, but Tex would only smile his great lopsided grin and never tell. Even though the real Effigy Goode was six years older, by the time he returned from overseas a flying ace, the two of them were so smitten it would have taken wild stallions to keep them apart.

Every Christmas Eve for many years to come, Alice would take a beautifully illustrated copy of *A Christmas Carol* from the bookshelf and read it to her children. Years later, she would read it to her grandchildren as well. By then, she was the last of the Book Battling Kids, an old lady with arthritis in her fingers and hair the color of winter frost. Alice didn't resemble the twelve-year-old girl who had hopped her first freight train in dirty overalls with her hair in pigtails in the autumn of 1935, but she remembered it all. Sometimes at night she still dreamed of flying.

Reading the book aloud by the fire was a special treat, one she saved for Christmas Eves alone. It brought back so many memories. She missed the ones who had gone before: her friends and family and Bob Cratchit, who had become like a second father to her. She often wondered if someday they would all be reunited in some special place where there was no difference between being real and being words on a page. She hoped so. What adventures they would have then!

She would stop while reading, sometimes more than once, with a tear in her eye. Then she would brush it away and smile as if it were such a simple thing. Her grandchildren never completely understood, but when Grammy Alice read the last line *'God bless us everyone'* and closed the book, she always wanted to be alone. Sitting with the book in her lap, she would stare for a long while out the window, watching the snow fall from the wispy dark clouds that hung so tenuous to Heaven.

About the Author

Richard Brian Harvell was born and raised in North Carolina, receiving his Bachelor's Degree in English from Appalachian State University in Boone. Taking the scenic tour the last ten years, he has lived in Atlanta, Houston, Chicago, and Los Angeles, but is back in the south where he plans to stay awhile (this makes his mother very happy). He has experimented with different genres, including some grisly horror for adults (we were too disturbed to read beyond the first chapter!), but this is his first foray into writing for middle readers. He wanted us to give a shout-out to his Carrin Terrier, RP, and his cat rescued from the Glendale, CA pound, Eukanuba.

Waterwood

Waterwood Publishing Group
PO Box 12540, Charlotte, NC 28220 USA.

Order Form

If you would like to purchase additional copies of *Adventures of the Book Battling Kids*, log on to our secure website at www.waterwoodpublishing.com and click on *How to Order*. You will be able to process the order using your PayPal account or a major credit card.

For postal orders, you may use the form below:

Please send the following title and quantities:

Adventures of the Book Battling Kids: _____

Quanity: _____

Name: _____

Address:_____

_____

City:_____

State:_____ Zip:_____

Telephone:_____

Email address:_____

Shipping by Air: **US:** $1.75 s/h. **International:** $3.50 s/h
Payment enclosed:
Cheque:_____   Money Order:_____

Clip, and mail this order form to:
Waterwood Publishing Group
PO Box 12540, Charlotte, NC 28220 USA.